Blake

Blake

Or, The Huts of America

Martin R. Delany

MINT EDITIONS

Blake: Or, The Huts of America was first published in 1859.

This edition published by Mint Editions 2021.

ISBN 9781513296852 | E-ISBN 9781513298351

Published by Mint Editions®

MINT
EDITIONS

minteditionbooks.com

Publishing Director: Jennifer Newens
Design & Production: Rachel Lopez Metzger
Project Manager: Micaela Clark
Typesetting: Westchester Publishing Services

Contents

Chapter 1

The Project

O n one of those exciting occasions during a contest for the presidency of the United States, a number of gentlemen met in the city of Baltimore. They were few in number, and appeared little concerned about the affairs of the general government. Though men of intelligence, their time and attention appeared to be entirely absorbed in an adventure of self-interest. They met for the purpose of completing arrangements for refitting the old ship "Merchantman," which then lay in the harbor near Fell's Point. Colonel Stephen Franks, Major James Armsted, Captain Richard Paul, and Captain George Royer composed those who represented the American side—Captain Juan Garcia and Captain Jose Castello, those of Cuban interest.

Here a conversation ensued upon what seemed a point of vital importance to the company; it related to the place best suited for the completion of their arrangements. The Americans insisted on Baltimore as affording the greatest facilities, and having done more for the encouragement and protection of the trade than any other known place, whilst the Cubans, on the other side, urged their objections on the ground that the continual increase of liberal principles in the various political parties, which were fast ushering into existence, made the objection beyond a controversy. Havana was contended for as a point best suited for adjusting their arrangements, and that too with many apparent reasons; but for some cause, the preference for Baltimore prevailed.

Subsequently to the adjustment of their affairs by the most complete arrangement for refitting the vessel, Colonel Franks took leave of the party for his home in the distant state of Mississippi.

Chapter 2

Colonel Franks at Home

On the return of Colonel Stephen Franks to his home at Natchez, he met there Mrs. Arabella, the wife of Judge Ballard, an eminent jurist of one of the Northern States. She had arrived but a day before him, on a visit to some relatives, of whom Mrs. Franks was one. The conversation, as is customary on the meeting of Americans residing in such distant latitudes, readily turned on the general policy of the country.

Mrs. Ballard possessed the highest intelligence, and Mrs. Maria Franks was among the most accomplished of Southern ladies.

"Tell me, Madam Ballard, how will the North go in the present issue?" enquired Franks.

"Give yourself no concern about that, Colonel," replied Mrs. Ballard, "you will find the North true to the country."

"What you consider true, may be false—that is, it might be true to you, and false to us," continued he.

"You do not understand me, Colonel," she rejoined, "we can have no interests separate from yours; you know the time-honored motto, 'united we stand,' and so forth, must apply to the American people under every policy in every section of the Union."

"So it should, but amidst the general clamor in the contest for ascendancy, may you not lose sight of this important point?"

"How can we? You, I'm sure, Colonel, know very well that in our country commercial interests have taken precedence of all others, which is a sufficient guarantee of our fidelity to the South."

"That may be, madam, but we are still apprehensive."

"Well, sir, we certainly do not know what more to do to give you assurance of our sincerity. We have as a plight of faith yielded Boston, New York, and Philadelphia—the intelligence and wealth of the North—in carrying out the Compromise measures for the interests of the South; can we do more?"

"True, Madam Ballard, true! I yield the controversy. You have already done more than we of the South expected. I now remember that the Judge himself tried the first case under the Act, in your city, by which the measures were tested."

"He did, sir, and if you will not consider me unwomanly by telling you, desired me, on coming here, to seek every opportunity to give the fullest assurance that the judiciary are sound on that question. Indeed, so far as an individual might be concerned, his interests in another direction—as you know—place him beyond suspicion," concluded Mrs. Ballard.

"I am satisfied, madam, and by your permission, arrest the conversation. My acknowledgements, madam!" bowed the Colonel, with true Southern courtesy.

"Maria, my dear, you look careworn; are you indisposed?" inquired Franks of his wife, who during conversation sat silent.

"Not physically, Colonel," replied she, "but—"

Just at this moment a servant, throwing open the door, announced dinner.

Besides a sprightly black boy of some ten years of age, there was in attendance a prepossessing, handsome maidservant, who generally kept, as much as the occasion would permit, behind the chair of her mistress. A mutual attachment appeared to exist between them, the maid apparently disinclined to leave the mistress, who seemed to keep her as near her person as possible.

Now and again the fat cook, Mammy Judy, would appear at the door of the dining room bearing a fresh supply for the table, who with a slight nod of the head, accompanied with an affectionate smile and the word "Maggie," indicated a tie much closer than that of mere fellow servants.

Maggie had long been the favorite maidservant of her mistress, having attained the position through merit. She was also nurse and foster mother to the two last children of Mrs. Franks, and loved them, to all appearance, as her own. The children reciprocated this affection, calling her "Mammy."

Mammy Judy, who for years had occupied this position, ceded it to her daughter; she preferring, in consequence of age, the less active life of the culinary department.

The boy Tony would frequently cast a comic look upon Mrs. Ballard, then imploringly gaze in the face of his mistress. So intent was he in this, that twice did his master admonish him by a nod of the head.

"My dear," said the Colonel, "you are dull today; pray tell me what makes you sad?"

"I am not bodily afflicted, Colonel Franks, but my spirit is heavy," she replied.

"How so? What is the matter?"

"That will be best answered at another time and place, Colonel."

Giving his head an unconscious scratch accompanied with a slight twitch of the corner of the mouth, Franks seemed to comprehend the whole of it.

On one of her Northern tours to the watering places—during a summer season some two years previous, having with her Maggie the favorite—Mrs. Franks visited the family of the Judge, at which time Mrs. Ballard first saw the maid. She was a dark mulatto of a rich, yellow, autumnlike complexion, with a matchless, cushionlike head of hair, neither straight nor curly, but handsomer than either.

Mrs. Franks was herself a handsome lady of some thirty-five summers, but ten years less in appearance, a little above medium height, between the majestic and graceful, raven-black hair, and dark, expressive eyes. Yet it often had been whispered that in beauty the maid equalled if not excelled the mistress. Her age was twenty-eight.

The conduct of Mrs. Franks toward her servant was more like that of an elder sister than a mistress, and the mistress and maid sometimes wore dresses cut from the same web of cloth. Mrs. Franks would frequently adjust the dress and see that the hair of her maid was properly arranged. This to Mrs. Ballard was as unusual as it was an objectionable sight, especially as she imagined there was an air of hauteur in her demeanor. It was then she determined to subdue her spirit.

Acting from this impulse, several times in her absence, Mrs. Ballard took occasion to administer to the maid severities she had never experienced at the hands of her mistress, giving her at one time a severe slap on the cheek, calling her an "impudent jade."

At this, Mrs. Franks, on learning, was quite surprised; but on finding that the maid gave no just cause for it, took no further notice of it, designedly evading the matter. But before leaving, Mrs. Ballard gave her no rest until she gave her the most positive assurance that she would part with the maid on her next visit to Natchez. And thus she is found pressing her suit at the residence of the Mississippi planter.

Chapter 3

THE FATE OF MAGGIE

After dinner Colonel Franks again pressed the inquiry concerning the disposition of his lady. At this time the maid was in the culinary department taking her dinner. The children having been served, she preferred the company of her old mother whom she loved, the children hanging around, and upon her lap. There was no servant save the boy Tony present in the parlor.

"I can't, I won't let her go! she's a dear good girl!" replied Mrs. Franks. "The children are attached to her, and so am I; let Minny or any other of them go—but do not, for Heaven's sake, tear Maggie from me!"

"Maria, my dear, you've certainly lost your balance of mind! Do try and compose yourself," admonished the Colonel. "There's certainly no disposition to do contrary to your desires; try and be a little reasonable."

"I'm sure, cousin, I see no cause for your importunity. No one that I know of designs to hurt the Negro girl. I'm sure it's not me!" impatiently remarked Mrs. Ballard.

During this, the boy had several times gone into the hall, looking toward the kitchen, then meaningly into the parlor as if something unusual were going on.

Mammy Judy becoming suspicious, went into the hall and stood close beside the parlor door, listening at the conversation.

"Cousin, if you will listen for a moment, I wish to say a word to you," said Mrs. Ballard. "The Judge, as you know, has a countryseat in Cuba near the city of Havana, where we design making every year our winter retreat. As we cannot take with us either free Negroes or white servants, on account of the existing restrictions, I must have a slave, and of course I prefer a well-trained one, as I know all yours to be. The price will be no object; as I know it will be none to you, it shall be none to me."

"I will not consent to part with her, cousin Arabella, and it is useless to press the matter any further!" emphatically replied Mrs. Franks.

"I am sure, cousin Maria, it was well understood between the Colonel and the Judge, that I was to have one of your best-trained maidservants!" continued Mrs. Ballard.

"The Colonel and the Judge! If any such understanding exist, it is without my knowledge and consent, and—"

"It is true, my dear," interposed the Colonel, "but—"

"Then," replied she, "heaven grant that I may go too! from—"

"Pah, pah! cousin Maria Franks, I'm really astonished at you to take on so about a Negro girl! You really appear to have lost your reason. I would not behave so for all the Negroes in Mississippi."

"My dear," said Franks, "I have been watching the conduct of that girl for some time past; she is becoming both disobedient and unruly, and as I have made it a rule of my life never to keep a disobedient servant, the sooner we part with her the better. As I never whip my servants, I do not want to depart from my rule in her case."

Maggie was true to her womanhood, and loyal to her mistress, having more than once communicated to her ears facts the sounds of which reflected no credit in his. For several repulses such as this, it was that she became obnoxious to her master.

"Cousin Maria, you certainly have forgotten; I'm sure, when last at the North, you promised in presence of the girl, that I was to have her, and I'm certain she's expecting it," explained Mrs. Ballard.

"This I admit," replied Mrs. Franks, "but you very well know, cousin Arabella, that that promise was a mere ruse, to reconcile an uneasiness which you informed me you discovered in her, after over-hearing a conversation between her and some free Negroes, at Saratoga Springs."

"Well, cousin, you can do as you please," concluded Mrs. Ballard.

"Colonel, I'm weary of this conversation. What am I to expect?" enquired Mrs. Franks.

"It's a settled point, my dear, she must be sold!" decisively replied Franks.

"Then I must hereafter be disrespected by our own slaves! You know, Colonel, that I gave my word to Henry, her husband, your most worthy servant, that his wife should be here on his return. He had some misgiving that she was to be taken to Cuba before his return, when I assured him that she should be here. How can I bear to meet this poor creature, who places every confidence in what we tell him? He'll surely be frantic."

"Nonsense, cousin, nonsense," sneered Mrs. Ballard. "Frantic, indeed! Why you speak of your Negro slaves as if speaking of equals.

MAKE HIM KNOW THAT WHATEVER you order, he must be contented with."

"I'll soon settle the matter with him, should he dare show any feelings about it!" interposed Franks. "When do you look for him, Maria?"

"I'm sure, Colonel, you know more about the matter than I do. Immediately after you left, he took the horses to Baton Rouge, where at the last accounts he was waiting the conclusion of the races. Judge Dilbreath had entered them according to your request—one horse for each day's races. I look for him every day. Then there are more than him to reconcile. There's old Mammy Judy, who will run mad about her. You know, Colonel, she thought so much of her, that she might be treated tenderly the old creature gave up her situation in the house as nurse and foster mother to our children, going into the kitchen to do the harder work."

"Well, my dear, we'll detain your cousin till he comes. I'll telegraph the Judge that, if not yet left, to start him home immediately."

"Colonel, that will be still worse, to let him witness her departure; I would much rather she'd leave before his return. Poor thing!" she sighed.

"Then she may go!" replied he.

"And what of poor old mammy and his boy?"

"I'll soon settle the matter with old Judy."

Mrs. Franks looking him imploringly in the face, let drop her head, burying her face in the palms of her hands. Soon it was found necessary to place her under the care of a physician.

Old Mammy Judy had long since beckoned her daughter, where both stood in breathless silence catching every word that passed.

At the conclusion, Maggie, clasping her hands, exclaimed in suppressed tones, "O mammy, O mammy! what shall I do? O, is there no hope for me? Can't you beg master—can't you save me!"

"Look to de Laud, my chile! Him ony able to bring yeh out mo' nah conkeh!" was the prayerful advice of the woe-stricken old mother. Both, hastening into the kitchen, falling upon their knees, invoked aloud the God of the oppressed.

Hearing in that direction an unusual noise, Franks hastened past the kitchen door, dropping his head, and clearing his throat as he went along. This brought the slaves to an ordinary mood, who trembled at his approach.

Chapter 4

Departure of Maggie

The countryseat of Franks, or the "great house" of the cotton plantation, was but a short distance from the city. Mrs. Franks, by the advice of her physician, was removed there to avoid the disturbance of the town, when at the same time Mrs. Ballard left with her slave Maggie en route for Baltimore, whither she designed leaving her until ready to sail for Cuba.

"Fahwell, my chile! fahwell; may God A'mighty be wid you!" were the parting words of the poor old slave, who with streaming eyes gazed upon her parting child for the last time.

"O mammy! Can't you save me? O Lord, what shall I do? O my husband! O my poor child! O my! O my!" were the only words, the sounds of which died upon the breeze, as the cab hastily bore her to a steamer then lying at the wharf.

Poor old Mammy Judy sat at the kitchen door with elbows resting upon her knee, side of the face resting in the palm of the hand, tears streaming down, with a rocking motion, noticing nothing about her, but in sorrow moaning just distinctly enough to be understood: "Po' me! Po' me! Po' me!"

The sight was enough to move the heart of anyone, and it so affected Franks that he wished he had "never owned a Negro."

Daddy Joe, the husband of Mammy Judy, was a field hand on the cotton place, visiting his wife at the town residence every Saturday night. Colonel Franks was a fine, grave, senatorial-looking man, of medium height, inclined to corpulency, black hair, slightly grey, and regarded by his slaves as a good master, and religiously as one of the best of men.

On their arrival at the great house, those working nearest gathered around the carriage, among whom was Daddy Joe.

"Wat a mautta wid missus?" was the general inquiry of the gang.

"Your mistress is sick, boys," replied the master.

"Maus, whah's Margot?" enquired the old man, on seeing his mistress carried into the house without the attendance of her favorite maidservant.

"She's in town, Joe," replied Franks.

"How's Judy, seh?"

"Judy is well."

"Tank'e seh!" politely concluded the old man, with a bow, turning away in the direction of his work—with a countenance expressive of anything but satisfaction—from the interview.

The slaves, from their condition, are suspicious; any evasion or seeming design at suppressing the information sought by them frequently arouses their greatest apprehension.

Not unfrequently the mere countenance, a look, a word, or laugh of the master, is an unerring foreboding of misfortune to the slave. Ever on the watch for these things, they learn to read them with astonishing precision.

This day was Friday, and the old slave consoled himself with the thought that on the next evening he would be able to see and know for himself the true state of things about his master's residence in town. The few hours intervening were spent with great anxiety, which was even observed by his fellow slaves.

At last came Saturday evening and with it, immediately after sunset, Daddy Joe made his appearance at the hall door of the great house, tarrying only long enough to inquire "How's missus?" and receive the reply, "she's better," when a few moments found him quite out of sight, striding his way down the lane toward the road to the city.

The sudden and unexpected fate of Maggie had been noised among the slaves throughout the entire neighborhood; many who had the opportunity of doing so, repairing to the house to learn the facts.

In the lower part of the town, bordering on the river there is a depot or receptacle for the slave gangs brought by professional traders. This part of the town is known as "Natchez-under-the-Hill." It is customary among the slaves when any of their number are sold, to say that they are gone "under the hill," and their common salutation through the day was that "Franks' Mag had gone under the hill."

As with quickened steps Daddy Joe approached the town, his most fearful apprehensions became terribly realized when meeting a slave who informed him that "Margot had gone under the hill." Falling upon his knees, in the fence corner, the old man raised his voice in supplication of Divine aid: "O Laud! dow has promis' in dine own wud, to be a fadah to de fadaless, an' husban to de widah! O Laud, let dy wud run an' be glorify! Sof'en de haud haut ob de presseh, an' let my po' chile cum back! an'—"

"Stop that noise there, old nigger!" ordered a patrol approaching him. "Who's boy are you?"

"Sahvant, mausta!" saluted the old slave, "I b'long to cunel Frank, seh!"

"Is this old Joe?"

"Dis is me maus Johnny."

"You had better trudge along home then, as it's likely old Judy wants to see you about this time."

"Tank'e seh," replied the old man, with a bow, feeling grateful that he was permitted to proceed.

"Devilish good, religious old Negro," he remarked to his associates, as the old man left them in the road.

A few minutes more, and Daddy Joe entered the kitchen door at his master's residence. Mammy Judy, on seeing him, gave vent afresh to bitter wailing, when the emotion became painfully mutual.

"O husban'! Husban'! Onah po' chile is gone!" exclaimed the old woman, clasping him around the neck.

"Laud! dy will be done!" exclaimed he. "Ole umin, look to de Laud! as he am suffishen fah all tings"; both, falling on their knees, breathed in silence their desires to God.

"How long! How long! O Laud how long!" was the supplicating cry of the old woman being overcome with devotion and sorrow.

Taking the little grandchild in his arms, "Po' chile," said the old man, "I wish yeh had nebeh been baun!" impressing upon it kisses whilst it slept.

After a fervant and earnest prayer to God for protection to themselves, little grandson Joe, the return of his mother their only child, and blessings upon their master and the recovery of their mistress, the poor old slaves retired to rest for the evening, to forget their sorrows in the respite of sleep.

Chapter 5

A Vacancy

This morning the sun rose with that beauty known to a Southern sky in the last month of autumn. The day was Sabbath, and with it was ushered in every reminiscence common to the customs of that day and locality.

That she might spend the day at church for the diversion of her mind, Mrs. Franks was brought in to her city residence; and Natchez, which is usually gay, seemed more so on this day than on former occasions.

When the bells began to signal the hour of worship, the fashionable people seemed en masse to crowd the streets. The carriages ran in every direction, bearing happy hearts and cheerful faces to the various places of worship—there to lay their offerings on the altar of the Most High for the blessings they enjoyed, whilst peering over every gate, out of every alley, or every kitchen door, could be seen the faithful black servants who, staying at home to prepare them food and attend to other domestic duties, were satisfied to look smilingly upon their masters and families as they rode along, without for a moment dreaming that they had a right to worship the same God, with the same promise of life and salvation.

"God bless you, missus! Pray fah me," was the honest request of many a simplehearted slave who dared not aspire to the enjoyment of praying for himself in the Temple of the living God.

But amidst these scenes of gaiety and pleasure, there was one much devoted to her church who could not be happy that day, as there to her was a seeming vacancy which could not be filled—the seat of her favorite maidservant. The Colonel, as a husband and father, was affectionate and indulgent; but his slave had offended, disobeyed his commands, and consequently, had to be properly punished, or he be disrespected by his own servants. The will of the master being absolute, his commands should be enforced, let them be what they may, and the consequences what they would. If slavery be right, the master is justifiable in enforcing obedience to his will; deny him this, and you at once deprive him of the right to hold a slave—the one is a necessary sequence of the other. Upon this principle Colonel Franks acted, and the premise justified the conclusion.

When the carriage drove to the door, Mrs. Franks wept out most bitterly, refusing to enter because her favorite maid could not be an incumbent. Fears being entertained of seriousness in her case, it was thought advisable to let her remain quietly at home.

Daddy Joe and Mammy Judy were anxious spectators of all that transpired at the door of the mansion, and that night, on retiring to their humble bed, earnestly petitioned at the altar of Grace that the Lord would continue upon her his afflictions until their master, convinced of his wrongs, would order the return of their child.

This the Colonel would have most willingly done without the petition of Joe or Judy, but the case had gone too far, the offense was too great, and consequently there could be no reconsideration.

"Poor things," muttered Mrs. Franks in a delirium, "she served him right! And this her only offense! Yes, she was true to me!"

Little Joe, the son of Maggie, in consequence of her position to the white children—from whom her separation had been concealed—had been constantly with his grandmother, and called her "mammy." Accustomed to being without her, he was well satisfied so long as permitted to be with the old woman Judy.

So soon as her condition would permit, Mrs. Franks was returned to her countryseat to avoid the contingencies of the city.

Chapter 6

Henry's Return

E arly on Monday morning, a steamer was heard puffing up the Mississippi. Many who reside near the river, by custom can tell the name of every approaching boat by the peculiar sound of the steampipe, the one in the present instance being the "Sultana."

Daddy Joe had risen and just leaving for the plantation, but stopped a moment to be certian.

"Hush!" admonished Mammy Judy. "Hush! Sho chile, do'n yeh heah how she hollah? Sholy dat's de wat's name! wat dat yeh call eh? 'Suckana,' wat not; sho! I ain' gwine bautha my head long so—sho! See, ole man see! Dah she come! See dat now! I tole yeh so, but yeh uden bleve me!" And the old man and woman stood for some minutes in breathless silence, although the boat must have been some five miles distant, as the escape of steam can be heard on the western waters a great way off.

The approach toward sunrise admonished Daddy Joe of demands for him at the cotton farm, when after bidding "good monin' ole umin," he hurried to the daily task which lay before him.

Mammy Judy had learned—by the boy Tony—that Henry was expected on the "Sultana," and at the approach of every steamer, her head had been thrust out of the door or window to catch a distinct sound. In motionless attitude after the departure of her husband this morning, the old woman stood awaiting the steamer, when presently the boat arrived. But then to be certain that it was the expected vessel— now came the suspense.

The old woman was soon relieved from this most disagreeable of all emotions, by the cry of newsboys returning from the wharf: "'Ere's the 'Picayune,' 'Atlas,' 'Delta'! Lates' news from New Orleans by the swift steamer 'Sultana'!"

"Dah now!" exclaimed Mammy Judy in soliloquy. "Dah now! I tole yeh so!—de wat's name come!" Hurrying into the kitchen, she waited with anxiety the arrival of Henry.

Busying about the breakfast for herself and other servants about the house—the white members of the family all being absent—Mammy

Judy for a time lost sight of the expected arrival. Soon however, a hasty footstep arrested her attention, when on looking around it proved to be Henry who came smiling up the yard.

"How'd you do, mammy! How's Mag' and the boy?" inquired he, grasping the old woman by the hand.

She burst into a flood of tears, throwing herself upon him.

"What is the matter!" exclaimed Henry. "Is Maggie dead?"

"No chile," with increased sobs she replied, "much betteh she wah."

"My God! Has she disgraced herself?"

"No chile, may be betteh she dun so, den she bin heah now an' not sole. Maus Stephen sell eh case she!—I dun'o, reckon dat's da reason."

"What!—Do you tell me, mammy, she had better disgraced herself than been sold! By the—!"

"So, Henry! yeh ain't gwine swah! hope yeh ain' gwine lose yeh 'ligion? Do'n do so; put yeh trus' in de Laud, he is suffishen fah all!"

"DON'T TELL ME ABOUT RELIGION! What's religion to me? My wife is sold away from me by a man who is one of the leading members of the very church to which both she and I belong! Put my trust in the Lord! I have done so all my life nearly, and of what use is it to me? My wife is sold from me just the same as if I didn't. I'll—"

"Come, come, Henry, yeh mus'n talk so; we is po' weak an' bline cretehs, an' cah see de way uh da Laud. He move' in a mystus way, his wundahs to puhfaum."

"So he may, and what is all that to me? I don't gain anything by it, and—"

"Stop, Henry, stop! Ain' de Laud bless yo' soul? Ain' he take yeh foot out de miah an' clay, an' gib yeh hope da uddah side dis vale ub teahs?"

"I'm tired looking the other side; I want a hope this side of the vale of tears. I want something on this earth as well as a promise of things in another world. I and my wife have been both robbed of our liberty, and you want me to be satisfied with a hope of heaven. I won't do any such thing; I have waited long enough on heavenly promises; I'll wait no longer. I—"

"Henry, wat de mauttah wid yeh? I neveh heah yeh talk so fo'—yeh sin in de sight ub God; yeh gone clean back, I reckon. De good Book tell us, a tousan' yeahs wid man, am but a day wid de Laud. Boy, yeh got wait de Laud own pinted time."

"Well, mammy, it is useless for me to stand here and have the same gospel preached into my ears by you, that I have all my life time heard from my enslavers. My mind is made up, my course is laid out, and if life last, I'll carry it out. I'll go out to the place today, and let them know that I have returned."

"Sho boy! What yeh gwine do, bun house down? Bettah put yeh trus' in de Laud!" concluded the old woman.

"You have too much religion, mammy, for me to tell you what I intend doing," said Henry in conclusion.

After taking up his little son, impressing on his lips and cheeks kisses for himself and tears for his mother, the intelligent slave left the abode of the careworn old woman, for that of his master at the cotton place.

Henry was a black—a pure Negro—handsome, manly and intelligent, in size comparing well with his master, but neither so fleshy nor heavy built in person. A man of good literary attainments—unknown to Colonel Franks, though he was aware he could read and write—having been educated in the West Indies, and decoyed away when young. His affection for wife and child was not excelled by Colonel Franks's for his. He was bold, determined and courageous, but always mild, gentle and courteous, though impulsive when an occasion demanded his opposition.

Going immediately to the place, he presented himself before his master. Much conversation ensued concerning the business which had been entrusted to his charge, all of which was satisfactorily transacted, and full explanations concerning the horses, but not a word was uttered concerning the fate of Maggie, the Colonel barely remarking "your mistress is unwell."

After conversing till a late hour, Henry was assigned a bed in the great house, but sleep was far from his eyes. He turned and changed upon his bed with restlessness and anxiety, impatiently awaiting a return of the morning.

Chapter 7

MASTER AND SLAVE

Early on Tuesday morning, in obedience to his master's orders, Henry was on his way to the city to get the house in readiness for the reception of his mistress, Mrs. Franks having improved in three or four days. Mammy Judy had not yet risen when he knocked at the door.

"Hi Henry! yeh heah ready! huccum yeh git up so soon; arter some mischif I reckon? Do'n reckon yeh arter any good!" saluted Mammy Judy.

"No, mammy," replied he, "no mischief, but like a good slave such as you wish me to be, come to obey my master's will, just what you like to see."

"Sho boy! none yeh nonsens'; huccum I want yeh bey maus Stephen? Git dat nonsens' in yeh head las' night long so, I reckon! Wat dat yeh gwine do now?"

"I have come to dust and air the mansion for their reception. They have sold my wife away from me, and who else would do her work?" This reply excited the apprehension of Mammy Judy.

"Wat yeh gwine do, Henry? Yeh arter no good; yeh ain' gwine 'tack maus Stephen, is yeh?"

"What do you mean, mammy, strike him?"

"Yes! Reckon yeh ain' gwine hit 'im?"

"Curse—!"

"Henry, Henry, membeh wat ye 'fess! Fah de Laud sake, yeh ain' gwine take to swahin?" interrupted the old woman.

"I make no profession, mammy. I once did believe in religion, but now I have no confidence in it. My faith has been wrecked on the stony hearts of such pretended Christians as Stephen Franks, while passing through the stormy sea of trouble and oppression! And—"

"Hay, boy! yeh is gittin high! Yeh call maussa 'Stephen'?"

"Yes, and I'll never call him 'master' again, except when compelled to do so."

"Bettah g'long ten' t' de house fo' wite folks come, an' nebeh mine talkin' 'bout fightin' 'long wid maus Stephen. Wat yeh gwine do wid white folks? Sho!"

"I don't intend to fight him, Mammy Judy, but I'll attack him concerning my wife, if the words be my last! Yes, I'll—!" and, pressing his lips to suppress the words, the outraged man turned away from the old slave mother with such feelings as only an intelligent slave could realize.

The orders of the morning were barely executed when the carriage came to the door. The bright eyes of the footboy Tony sparkled when he saw Henry approaching the carriage.

"Well, Henry! Ready for us?" enquired his master.

"Yes, sir," was the simple reply. "Mistress!" he saluted, politely bowing as he took her hand to assist her from the carriage.

"Come, Henry my man, get out the riding horses," ordered Franks after a little rest.

"Yes, sir."

A horse for the Colonel and lady each was soon in readiness at the door, but none for himself, it always having been the custom in their morning rides, for the maid and manservant to accompany the mistress and master.

"Ready, did you say?" enquired Franks on seeing but two horses standing at the stile.

"Yes, sir."

"Where's the other horse?"

"What for, sir?"

"What for? Yourself, to be sure!"

"Colonel Franks!" said Henry, looking him sternly in the face. "When I last rode that horse in company with you and lady, my wife was at my side, and I will not now go without her! Pardon me—my life for it, I won't go!"

"Not another word, you black imp!" exclaimed Franks, with an uplifted staff in a rage, "or I'll strike you down in an instant!"

"Strike away if you will, sir, I don't care—I won't go without my wife!"

"You impudent scoundrel! I'll soon put an end to your conduct! I'll put you on the auction block, and sell you to the Negro-traders."

"Just as soon as you please sir, the sooner the better, as I don't want to live with you any longer!"

"Hold your tongue, sir, or I'll cut it out of your head! You ungrateful black dog! Really, things have come to a pretty pass when I must take impudence off my own Negro! By gracious!—God forgive me for the expression—I'll sell every Negro I have first! I'll dispose of him to the hardest Negro-trader I can find!" said Franks in a rage.

"You may do your mightiest, Colonel Franks. I'm not your slave, nor never was and you know it! And but for my wife and her people, I never would have stayed with you till now. I was decoyed away when young, and then became entangled in such domestic relations as to induce me to remain with you; but now the tie is broken! I know that the odds are against me, but never mind!"

"Do you threaten me, sir! Hold your tongue, or I'll take your life instantly, you villain!"

"No, sir, I don' threaten you, Colonel Franks, but I do say that I won't be treated like a dog. You sold my wife away from me, after always promising that she should be free. And more than that, you sold her because—! And now you talk about whipping me. Shoot me, sell me, or do anything else you please, but don't lay your hands on me, as I will not suffer you to whip me!"

Running up to his chamber, Colonel Franks seized a revolver, when Mrs. Franks, grasping hold of his arm, exclaimed, "Colonel! what does all this mean?"

"Mean, my dear? It's rebellion! A plot—this is but the shadow of a could that's fast gathering around us! I see it plainly, I see it!" responded the Colonel, starting for the stairs.

"Stop, Colonel!" admonished his lady. "I hope you'll not be rash. For Heaven's sake, do not stain your hands in blood!"

"I do not mean to, my dear! I take this for protection!" Franks hastening down stairs, when Henry had gone into the back part of the premises.

"Dah now! Dah now!" exclaimed Mammy Judy as Henry entered the kitchen. "See wat dis gwine back done foh yeh! Bettah put yo' trus' in de Laud! Henry, yeh gone clean back t' de wuhl ghin, yeh knows it!"

"You're mistaken, Mammy; I do trust the Lord as much as ever, but I now understand him better than I use to, that's all. I dont intend to be made a fool of any longer by false preaching."

"Henry!" interrogated Daddy Joe—who, apprehending difficulties in the case, had managed to get back to the house. "Yeh gwine lose all yo' 'ligion? Wat yeh mean, boy!"

"Religion!" replied Henry rebukingly. "That's always the cry with black people. Tell me nothing about religion when the very man who hands you the bread at communion has sold your daughter away from you!"

"Den yeh 'fen' God case man 'fen' yeh! Take cah, Henry, take cah! mine wat yeh 'bout; God is lookin' at yeh, an' if yeh no' willin' trus' 'im, yeh need'n call on 'im in time o' trouble."

"I dont intend, unless He does more for me then than He has done before. 'Time of need!' If ever man needed His assistance, I'm sure I need it now."

"Yeh do'n know wat yeh need; de Laud knows bes'. On'y trus' in 'im, an' 'e bring yeh out mo' nah conkah. By de help o' God I's heah dis day, to gib yeh cumfut!"

"I have trusted in Him, Daddy Joe, all my life, as I told Mammy Judy this morning, but—"

"Ah boy, yeh's gwine back! Dat on't do Henry, dat on't do!"

"Going back from what? My oppressor's religion! If I could only get rid of his inflictions as easily as I can his religion, I would be this day a free man, when you might then talk to me about 'trusting.'"

"Dis, Henry, am one uh de ways ob de Laud; 'e fus 'flicks us an' den he bless us."

"Then it's a way I don't like."

"Mine how yeh talk, boy! 'God moves in a myst'us way His wundahs to pehfaum,' an—"

"He moves too slow for me, Daddy Joe; I'm tired waiting so—"

"Come Henry, I hab no sich talk like dat! yeh is gittin' rale weaked; yeh gwine let de debil take full 'session on yeh! Take cah boy, mine how yeh talk!"

"It is not wickedness, Daddy Joe; you don't understand these things at all. If a thousand years with us is but a day with God, do you think that I am required to wait all that time?"

"Don't, Henry, don't! De wud say 'stan' still an' see de salbation.'"

"That's no talk for me, Daddy Joe; I've been 'standing still' long enough—I'll 'stand still' no longer."

"Den yeh no call t' bey God wud? Take cah boy, take cah!"

"Yes I have, and I intend to obey it, but that part was intended for the Jews, a people long since dead. I'll obey that intended for me."

"How yeh gwine bey it?"

"'Now is the accepted time, today is the day of salvation.' So you see, Daddy Joe, this is very different to standing still."

"Ah boy, I's feahd yeh's losen yeh 'ligion!"

"I tell you once for all, Daddy Joe, that I'm not only 'losing' but I have altogether lost my faith in the religion of my oppressors. As they are our religious teachers, my estimate of the thing they give is no greater than it is for those who give it."

With elbows upon his knees, and face resting in the palms of his hands, Daddy Joe for some time sat with his eyes steadily fixed on the floor, whilst Ailcey who for a part of the time had been an auditor to the conversation, went into the house about her domestic duties.

"Never mind, Henry! I hope it will not always be so with you. You have been kind and faithful to me and the Colonel, and I'll do anything I can for you!" sympathetically said Mrs. Franks, who, having been a concealed spectator of the interview between Henry and the old people, had just appeared before them.

Wiping away the emblems of grief which stole down his face, with a deep-toned voice upgushing from the recesses of a more than iron-pierced soul, he enquired, "Madam, what can you do! Where is my wife?" To this, Mrs. Franks gave a deep sigh. "Never mind, never mind!" continued he, "yes, I will mind, and by—!"

"O! HENRY, I HOPE YOU'VE not taken to swearing! I do hope you will not give over to wickedness! Our afflictions should only make our faith the stronger."

"'Wickedness.' Let the righteous correct the wicked, and the Christian condemn the sinner!"

"That is uncharitable in you, Henry! As you know I have always treated you kindly, and God forbid that I should consider myself any less than a Christian! And I claim as much at least for the Colonel, though like frail mortals he is liable to err at times."

"Madam!" said he with suppressed emotion—starting back a pace or two—"Do you think there is anything either in or out of hell so wicked, as that which Colonel Franks has done to my wife, and now about to do to me? For myself I care not—my wife!"

"Henry!" said Mrs. Franks, gently placing her hand upon his shoulder. "There is yet a hope left for you, and you will be faithful enough, I know, not to implicate any person. It is this: Mrs. Van Winter, a true friend of your race, is shortly going to Cuba on a visit, and I will arrange with her to purchase you through an agent on the day of your sale, and by that means you can get to Cuba, where probably you may be fortunate enough to get the master of your wife to become your purchaser."

"Then I have two chances!" replied Henry.

Just then Ailcey, thrusting her head in the door, requested the presence of her mistress in the parlor.

Chapter 8

The Sale

"Dah now, dah now!" exclaimed Mammy Judy. "Jis wat ole man been tellin' on yeh! Yeh go out yandah, yeh kick up yeh heel, git yeh head clean full proclamation an' sich like dat, an' let debil fool yeh, den go fool long wid wite folks long so, sho! Bettah go 'bout yeh bisness; been sahvin' God right, yeh no call t'do so eh reckon!"

"I don't care what comes! my course is laid out and my determination fixed, and nothing they can do can alter it. So you and Daddy Joe, mammy, had just as well quit your preaching to me the religion you have got from your oppressors."

"Soul-driveh git yeh, yeh cah git way fom dem eh doh recken! Sho chile, yeh ain' dat mighty!" admonished Mammy Judy.

"Henry, my chile, look to de Laud! Look to de Laud! Case 'e 'lone am able t' bah us up in ouah trouble! An—"

"Go directly sir, to Captain John Harris' office and ask him to call immediately to see me at my house!" ordered Franks.

Politely bowing, Henry immediately left the premises on his errand.

"Laud a' messy maus Stephen!" exclaimed Mammy Judy, on hearing the name of John Harris the Negro-trader. "Hope yeh arteh no haum! Gwine sell all on us to de tradehs?"

"Hoot-toot, hoot-toot! Judy, give yourself no uneasiness about that till you have some cause for it. So you and Joe may rest contented, Judy," admonished Franks.

"Tank'e maus Stephen! Case ah heahn yeh tell Henry dat yeh sell de las' nig—"

"Hush, ole umin, hush! Yeh tongue too long! Put yeh trus' in de Laud!" interrupted Daddy Joe.

"I treat my black folks well," replied Franks, "and all they have to—"

Here the doorbell having been rung, he was interrupted with a message from Ailcey, that a gentleman awaited his presence in the parlor.

At the moment which the Colonel left the kitchen, Henry stepped over the stile into the yard, which at once disclosed who the gentleman was to whom the master had been summoned. Henry passed directly around and behind the house.

"See, ole man, see! Reckon 'e gwine dah now!" whispered Mammy Judy, on seeing Henry pass through the yard without going into the kitchen.

"Whah?" enquired Daddy Joe.

"Dun'o out yandah, whah 'e gwine way from wite folks!" she replied.

The interview between Franks and the trader Harris was not over half an hour duration, the trader retiring, Franks being prompt and decisive in all of his transactions, making little ceremony.

So soon as the front door was closed, Ailcey smiling bore into the kitchen a half-pint glass of brandy, saying that her master had sent it to the old people.

The old man received it with compliments to his master, pouring it into a black jug in which there was both tansy and garlic, highly recommending it as a "bitters" and certain antidote for worms, for which purpose he and the old woman took of it as long as it lasted, though neither had been troubled with that particular disease since the days of their childhood.

"Wat de gwine do wid yeh meh son?" enquired Mammy Judy as Henry entered the kitchen.

"Sell me to the soul-drivers! what else would they do?"

"Yeh gwin 'tay 'bout till de git yeh?"

"I shant move a step! and let them do their—"

"Maus wants to see yeh in da front house, Henry," interrupted Ailcey, he immediately obeying the summons.

"Heah dat now!" said mammy Judy, as Henry followed the maid out of the kitchen.

"Carry this note, sir, directly to Captain Jack Harris!" ordered Franks, handing to Henry a sealed note. Receiving it, he bowed politely, going out of the front door, directly to the slave prison of Harris.

"Eh heh! I see," said Harris on opening the note, "Colonel Frank's boy; walk in here," passing through the office into a room which proved to be the first department of the slave prison. "No common Negro, I see! You're a shade higher. A pretty deep shade too! Can read, write, cipher; a good religious fellow, and has a Christian and sir name. The devil you say! Who's your father? Can you preach?"

"I have never tried," was the only reply.

"Have you ever been a member of Congress?" continued Harris with ridicule.

To this Henry made no reply.

"Wont answer, hey! Beneath your dignity. I understand that you're of that class of gentry who dont speak to common folks! You're not quite well enough dressed for a gentleman of your cloth. Here! Mr. Henry, I'll present you with a set of ruffles: give yourself no trouble sir, as I'll dress you! I'm here for that purpose," said Harris, fastening upon the wrists of the manly bondman a heavy pair of handcuffs.

"You hurt my wrist!" admonished Henry.

"New clothing will be a little tight when first put on. Now sir!" continued the trader, taking him to the back door and pointing into the yard at the slave gang there confined. "As you have been respectably dressed, walk out and enjoy yourself among the ladies and gentlemen there; you'll find them quite a select company."

Shortly after this the sound of the bellringer's voice was heard—a sound which usually spread terror among the slaves: "Will be sold this afternoon at three o'clock by public outcry, at the slave prison of Captain John Harris, a likely choice Negro fellow, the best trained body servant in the state, trained to the business by the most accomplished lady and gentleman Negro-trainers in the Mississippi Valley. Sale positive without a proviso."

"Dah, dah! Did'n eh tell yeh so? Ole man, ole man! heah dat now! Come heah. Dat jis what I been tellin on im, but 'e uden bleve me!" ejaculated old Mammy Judy on hearing the bell ring and the handbill read.

Falling upon their knees, the two old slaves prayed fervently to God, thanking him that it was as "well with them" as it was.

"Bless de Laud! My soul is happy!" cried out Mammy Judy being overcome with devotion, clapping her hands.

"Tang God, fah wat I feels in my soul!" responded Daddy Joe.

Rising from their knees with tears trickling down their cheeks, the old slaves endeavored to ease their troubled souls by singing,

> *Oh, when shall my sorrows subside,*
> *And when shall my troubles be ended;*
> *And when to the bosom of Christ be conveyed,*
> *To the mansions of joy and bliss;*
> *To the mansions of joy and bliss!*

"Wuhthy to be praise! Blessed be de name uh de Laud! Po' black folks, de Laud o'ny knows sats t' come ob us!" exclaimed Mammy Judy.

"Look to de Laud ole umin, 'e's able t' bah us out mo' neh conkeh. Keep de monin' stah in sight!" advised Daddy Joe.

"Yes, ole man, yes, dat I done dis many long day, an' ah ain' gwine lose sight uh it now! No, God bein' my helpeh, I is gwine keep my eyes right on it, dat I is!"

As the hour of three drew near, many there were going in the direction of the slave prison, a large number of persons having assembled at the sale.

"Draw near, gentlemen, draw near!" cried Harris. "The hour of sale is arrived: a positive sale with no proviso, cash down, or no sale at all!" A general laugh succeeded the introduction of the auctioneer.

"Come up here my lad!" continued the auctioneer, wielding a long red rawhide. "Mount this block, stand beside me, an' let's see which is the best looking man! We have met before, but I never had the pleasure of introducing you. Gentlemen one and all, I take pleasure in introducing to you Henry—pardon me, sir—Mr. Henry Holland, I believe—am I right, sir?—Mr. Henry Holland, a good looking fellow you will admit.

"I am offered one thousand dollars; one thousand dollars for the best looking Negro in all Mississippi! If all the negro boys in the state was as good looking as him, I'd give two thousand dollars for 'em all myself!" This caused another laugh. "Who'll give me one thousand five—"

Just then a shower of rain came on.

"Gentlemen!" exclaimed the auctioneer. "Without a place can be obtained large enough to shelter the people here assembled, the sale will have to be postponed. This is a proviso we couldn't foresee, an' therefore is not responsible for it." There was another hearty laugh.

A whisper went through the crowd, when presently a gentleman came forward, saying that those concerned had kindly tendered the use of the church which stood nearby, in which to continue the sale.

"Here we are again, gentlemen! Who bids five hundred more for the likely Negro fellow? I am offered fifteen hundred dollars for the finest Negro servant in the state! Come, my boy, bestir yourself an' don't stan' there like a statute; can't you give us a jig? whistle us a song! I forgot, the Negro fellow is religious; by the by, an excellent recommendation, gentlemen. Perhaps he'll give us a sermon. Say, git up there old fellow, an' hold forth. Can't you give us a sermon on Abolition? I'm only offered fifteen hundred dollars for the likely Negro boy! Fifteen, sixteen, sixteen hundred, just agoing at—eighteen, eighteen, nineteen hundred, nineteen hundred! Just agoing at nineteen hundred dollars for the best body servant in the state; just agoing at nineteen and without a better bid I'll—Going! Going! Go—!"

Just at this point a note was passed up the aisle to the auctioneer, who after reading it said, "Gentlemen! Circumstances beyond my control make it necessary that the sale be postponed until one day next week; the time of continuance will be duly announced," when, bowing, he left the stand.

"That's another proviso not in the original bill!" exclaimed a voice as the auctioneer left the stand, at which there were peals of laughter.

To secure himself against contingency, Harris immediately delivered Henry over to Franks.

There were present at the sale, Crow, Slider, Walker, Borbridge, Simpson, Hurst, Spangler and Williams, all noted slave traders, eager to purchase, some on their return home, and some with their gangs en route for the Southern markets.

The note handed the auctioneer read thus:

CAPT. HARRIS

Having learned that there are private individuals at the sale, who design purchasing my Negro man, Harry, for his own personal advantage, you will peremptorily postpone the sale—making such apology as the occasion demands—and effect a private sale with Richard Crow, Esq., who offers me two thousand dollars for him. Let the boy return to me. Believe me to be,

Very Respectfully,
STEPHEN FRANKS

Capt. John Harris. Natchez, Nov. 29th, 1852.

"Now, sir," said Franks to Henry, who had barely reached the house from the auction block, "take this pass and go to Jackson and Woodville, or anywhere else you wish to see your friends, so that you be back against Monday afternoon. I ordered a postponement of the sale, thinking that I would try you awhile longer, as I never had cause before to part with you. Now see if you can't be a better boy!"

Eagerly taking the note, thanking him with a low bow, turning away, Henry opened the paper, which read:

Permit the bearer my boy Henry, sometimes calling himself Henry Holland—a kind of negro pride he has—to pass and repass wherever he wants to go, he behaving himself properly.

STEPHEN FRANKS

To all whom it may concern. Natchez, Nov. 29th, 1852.

Carefully depositing the charte volante in his pocket wallet, Henry quietly entered the hut of Mammy Judy and Daddy Joe.

Chapter 9

The Runaway

D e Laud's good—bless his name!" exclaimed Mammy Judy wringing her hands as Henry entered their hut. "'e heahs de prahs ob 'is chilen. Yeh hab reason t' tang God yeh is heah dis day!"

"Yes Henry, see wat de Laud's done fah yeh. 'Tis true's I's heah dis day! Tang God fah dat!" added Daddy Joe.

"I think," replied he, after listening with patience to the old people, "I have reason to thank our Ailcey and Van Winter's Biddy; they, it seems to me, should have some credit in the matter."

"Sho boy, g'long whah yeh gwine! Yo' backslidin' gwine git yeh in trouble ghin eh reckon?" replied Mammy Judy.

Having heard the conversation between her mistress and Henry, Ailcey, as a secret, informed Van Winter's Derba, who informed her fellow servant Biddy, who imparted it to her acquaintance Nelly, the slave of esquire Potter, Nelly informing her mistress, who told the 'Squire, who led Franks into the secret of the whole matter.

"Mus'n blame me, Henry!" said Ailcey in an undertone. "I did'n mean de wite folks to know wat I tole Derba, nor she di'n mean it nuther, but dat devil, Pottah's Nell! us gals mean da fus time we ketch uh out, to duck uh in da rivah! She's rale wite folk's nigga, dat's jus' wat she is. Nevah mine, we'll ketch her yit!"

"I don't blame you Ailcey, nor either of Mrs. Van Winter's girls, as I know that you are my friends, neither of whom would do anything knowingly to injure me. I know Ailcey that you are a good girl, and believe you would tell me—"

"Yes Henry, I is yo' fren' an' come to tell yeh now wat da wite folks goin' to do."

"What is it Ailcey; what do you know?"

"Wy dat ugly ole devil Dick Crow—God fah gim me! But I hate 'im so, case he nothin' but po' wite man, no how—I know 'im he come from Fagina on—"

"Never mind his origin, Ailcey, tell me what you know concerning his visit in the house."

MARTIN R. DELANY

"I is goin' to, but da ugly ole devil, I hates 'im so! Maus Stephen had 'im in da pahla, an' 'e sole yeh to 'im, dat ugly ole po' wite devil, fah—God knows how much—a hole heap a money; 'two' somethin'."

"I know what it was, two thousand dollars, for that was his selling price to Jack Harris."

"Yes, dat was da sum, Henry."

"I am satisfied as to how much he can be relied on. Even was I to take the advice of the old people here, and become reconciled to drag out a miserable life of degradation and bondage under them, I would not be permitted to do so by this man, who seeks every opportunity to crush out my lingering manhood, and reduce my free spirit to the submission of a slave. He cannot do it, I will not submit to it, and I defy his power to make me submit."

"Laus a messy, Henry, yeh free man! huccum yeh not tell me long'o? Sho boy, bettah go long whah yeh gwine, out yandah, an' not fool long wid wite folks!" said Mammy Judy with surprise, "wat bring yeh heah anyhow?"

"That's best known to myself, mammy."

"Wat make yeh keep heah so long den, dat yeh ain' gone fo' dis?"

"Your questions become rather pressing, mammy; I can't tell you that either."

"Laud, Laud, Laud! So yeh free man? Well, well, well!"

"Once for all, I now tell you old people what I never told you before, nor never expected to tell you under such circumstances; that I never intend to serve any white man again. I'll die first!"

"De Laud a' messy on my po' soul! An' huccum yeh not gone befo'?"

"Carrying out the principles and advice of you old people 'standing still, to see the salvation.' But with me, 'now is the accepted time, today is the day of salvation.'"

"Well, well, well!" sighed Mammy Judy.

"I am satisfied that I am sold, and the wretch who did it seeks to conceal his perfidy by deception. Now if ever you old people did anything in your lives, you must do it now."

"Wat dat yeh want wid us?"

"Why, if you'll go, I'll take you on Saturday night, and make our escape to a free country."

"Wat place yeh call dat?"

"Canada!" replied Henry, with emotion.

"How fah yeh gwine take me?" earnestly enquired the old woman.

"I can't just now tell the distance, probably some two or three thousand miles from here, the way we'd have to go."

"De Laus a messy on me! An' wat yeh gwine do wid little Joe; ain gwine leave 'im behine?"

"No, Mammy Judy, I'd bury him in the bottom of the river first! I intend carrying him in a bundle on my back, as the Indians carry their babies."

"Wat yeh gwine do fah money; yeh ain' gwine rob folks on de road?"

"No mammy, I'll starve first. Have you and Daddy Joe saved nothing from your black-eye peas and poultry selling for many years?"

"Ole man, how much in dat pot undeh de flo' dah; how long since yeh count it?"

"Don'o," replied Daddy Joe, "las' time ah count it, da wah faughty guinea uh sich a mauttah, an' ah put in some six-seven guinea mo' since dat."

"Then you have some two hundred and fifty dollars in money."

"Dat do yeh?" enquired Mammy Judy.

"Yes, that of itself is enough, but—"

"Den take it an' go long whah yeh gwine; we ole folks too ole fah gwine headlong out yandah an' don'o whah we gwine. Sho boy! take de money an' g'long!" decisively replied the old woman after all her inquisitiveness.

"If you don't know, I do, mammy, and that will answer for all."

"Dat ain' gwine do us. We ole folks ain' politishon an' undestan' de graumma uh dese places, an' w'en we git dah den maybe do'n like it an cahn' git back. Sho chile, so long whah yeh gwine!"

"What do you say, Daddy Joe? Whatever you have to say, must be said quick, as time with me is precious."

"We is too ole dis time a day, chile, t'go way out yauah de Laud knows whah; bettah whah we is."

"You'll not be too old to go if these whites once take a notion to sell you. What will you do then?"

"Trus' to de Laud!"

"Yes, the same old slave song—'Trust to the Lord.' Then I must go, and—"

"Ain' yeh gwine take de money, Henry?" interrupted the old woman.

"No, mammy, since you will not go, I leave it for you and Daddy Joe, as you may yet have use for it, or those may desire to use it who better understand what use to make of it than you and Daddy Joe seem willing to be instructed in."

"Den yeh 'ont have de money?"

"I thank you and Daddy most kindly, Mammy Judy, for your offer, and only refuse because I have two hundred guineas about me."

"Sho boy, yeh got all dat, no call t'want dat little we got. Whah yeh git all dat money? Do'n reckon yeh gwine tell me! Did'n steal from maus Stephen, do'n reckon?"

"No, mammy, I'm incapable of stealing from any one, but I have, from time to time, taken by littles, some of the earnings due me for more than eighteen years' service to this man Franks, which at the low rate of two hundred dollars a year, would amount to sixteen hundred dollars more than I secured, exclusive of the interest, which would have more than supplied my clothing, to say nothing of the injury done me by degrading me as a slave. 'Steal' indeed! I would that when I had an opportunity, I had taken fifty thousand instead of two. I am to understand you old people as positively declining to go, am I?"

"No, no, chile, we cahn go! We put ouh trus' in de Laud, he bring us out mo' nah conkah."

"Then from this time hence, I become a runaway. Take care of my poor boy while he's with you. When I leave the swamps, or where I'll go, will never be known to you. Should my boy be suddenly missed, and you find three notches cut in the bark of the big willow tree, on the side away from your hut, then give yourself no uneasiness; but if you don't find these notches in the tree, then I know nothing about him. Goodbye!" And Henry strode directly for the road to Woodville.

"Fahwell me son, fahwell, an' may God a'mighty go wid you! May de Laud guide an' 'tect yeh on de way!"

The child, contrary to his custom, commenced crying, desiring to see Mamma Maggie and Dadda Henry. Every effort to quiet him was unavailing. This brought sorrow to the old people's hearts and tears to their eyes, which they endeavored to soothe in a touching lamentation:

> *See wives and husbands torn apart,*
> *Their children's screams, they grieve my heart.*
> *They are torn away to Georgia!*
> *Come and go along with me—*
> *They are torn away to Georgia!*
> *Go sound the Jubilee!*

Chapter 10

Merry Making

T he day is Saturday, a part of which is given by many liberal masters to their slaves, the afternoon being spent as a holiday, or in vending such little marketable commodities as they might by chance possess.

As a token of gratitude, it is customary in many parts of the South for the slaves to invite their masters to their entertainments. This evening presented such an occasion on the premises of Colonel Stephen Franks.

This day Mammy Judy was extremely busy, for in addition to the responsibility of the culinary department, there was her calico habit to be done up—she would not let Potter's Milly look any better than herself—and an old suit of the young master George's clothes had to be patched and darned a little before little Joe could favorably compare with Craig's Sooky's little Dick. And the cast-off linen given to her husband for the occasion might require a "little doing up."

"Wat missus sen' dis shut heah wid de bres all full dis debilment an' nonsense fah?" said Mammy Judy, holding up the garment, looking at the ruffles. "Sho! Missus mus' be crack, sen' dis heah! Ole man ain' gwine sen' he soul to de ole boy puttin' on dis debilment!" And she hastened away with the shirt, stating to her mistress her religious objections. Mrs. Franks smiled as she took the garment, telling her that the objections could be easily removed by taking off the ruffles.

"Dat look sumphen like!" remarked the old woman, when Ailcey handed her the shirt with the ruffles removed.

"Sen' dat debilment an' nonsense heah! Sho!" And carrying it away smiling, she laid it upon the bed.

The feast of the evening was such as Mammy Judy was capable of preparing when in her best humor, consisting of all the delicacies usually served up on the occasion of corn huskings in the graingrowing region.

Conscious that he was not entitled to their gratitude, Colonel Franks declined to honor the entertainment, though the invitation was a ruse to deceive him, as he had attempted to deceive them.

The evening brought with it much of life's variety, as may be seen among the slave population of the South. There were Potter's slaves,

MARTIN R. DELANY

and the people of Mrs. Van Winter, also those of Major Craig, and Dr. Denny, all dressed neatly, and seemingly very happy.

Ailcey was quite the pride of the evening, in an old gauze orange dress of her mistress, and felt that she deserved to be well thought of, as proving herself the friend of Henry, the son-in-law of Daddy Joe and Mammy Judy, the heads of the entertainment. Mammy Judy and Potter's Milly were both looking matronly in their calico gowns and towlinen aprons, and Daddy Joe was the honored and observed of the party, in an old black suit with an abundance of surplus.

"He'p yeh se'f, chilen!" said Mammy Judy, after the table had been blessed by Daddy Joe. "Henry ain' gwine be heah, 'e gone to Woodville uh some whah dah, kick'n up 'e heel. Come, chilen, eat haughty, mo' whah dis come f'om. He'p yeh se'f now do'n—"

"I is, Aun' Judy; I likes dis heah kine a witals!" drawled out Potter's Nelse, reaching over for the fifth or sixth time. "Dis am good shaut cake!"

"O mammy, look at Jilson!" exclaimed Ailcey, as a huge, rough field hand—who refused to go to the table with the company, but sat sulkily by himself in one corner—was just walking away, with two whole "cakes" of bread under his arm.

"WAT YEH GWINE DO WID dat bread, Jilson?" enquired the old woman.

"I gwine eat it, dat wat I gwine do wid it! I ain' had no w'eat bread dis two hauvest!" he having come from Virginia, where such articles of food on harvest occasion were generally allowed the slave.

"Big hog, so 'e is!" rebukingly said Ailcey, when she saw that Jilson was determined in his purpose.

"Nebeh mine dat childen, plenty mo'!" responded Mammy Judy.

"Ole umin, dat chile in de way dah; de gals haudly tu'n roun'," suggested Daddy Joe, on seeing the pallet of little Joe crowded upon as the girls were leaving the table, seating themselves around the room.

"Ailcey, my chile, jes' run up to de hut wid 'im, 'an lay 'im in de bed; ef yeh fuhd, Van Wintah' Ben go wid yeh; ah knows 'e likes to go wid de gals," said Mammy Judy.

Taking up his hat with a bland smile, Ben obeyed orders without a demur.

The entertainment was held at the extreme end of a two-acre lot in the old slave quarters, while the hut of Mammy Judy was near the great house. Ailcey thought she espied a person retreat into the shrubbery and, startled, she went to the back door of the hut, but Ben hooted at the idea of any person out and about on such an occasion, except indeed it was Jilson with his bread. The child being carefully placed in bed, Ailcey and her protector were soon mingled with the merry slaves.

There were three persons generally quite prominent among the slaves of the neighborhood, missed on this occasion; Franks' Charles, Denny's Sam, and Potter's Andy; Sam being confined to bed by sickness.

"Ailcey, whah's Chaules—huccum 'e not heah?" enquired Mammy Judy.

"Endeed, I dun'o mammy."

"Huccum Pottah's Andy ain' heah muddah?"

"Andy a' home tonight, Aun' Judy, an' uh dun'o whah 'e is," replied Winny.

"Gone headlong out yandah, arteh no good, uh doh reckon, an' Chaules 'e gone dah too," replied the old woman.

"Da ain' nothin' mattah wid dis crowd, Aun' Judy," complimented Nelse as he sat beside Derba. At this expression Mammy Judy gave a deep sigh, on the thought of her absent daughter.

"Come, chilen," suggested Mammy Judy, "yeh all eat mighty hauty, an' been mighty merry, an' 'joy yehse'f much; we now sing praise to de Laud fah wat 'e done fah us," raising a hymn in which all earnestly joined:

Oh! Jesus, Jesus is my friend,
He'll be my helper to the end, . . .

"Young folk, yeh all bettah git ready now an' go, fo' de patrollas come out. Yeh all 'joy yeh se'f much, now time yeh gone. Hope yeh all sauv God Sunday. Ole man fo' de all gone, hab wud uh prah," advised the old woman; the following being sung in conclusion:

The Lord is here, and the Lord is all around us;
Canaan, Canaan's a very happy home—
O, glory! O, glory! O, glory! God is here,

when the gathering dispersed, the slaves going cheerfully to their homes.

"Come ole man, yeh got mautch? light sum dem shavens dah, quick. Ah cah fine de chile heah on dis bed!" said Mammy Judy, on entering the hut and feeling about in the dark for little Joe. "Ailcey, wat yeh done wid de chile?"

"E's dah, Mammy Judy, I lain 'im on de bed, ah spose 'e roll off." The shavings being lit, here was no child to be found.

"My Laud, ole man! whah's de chile? Wat dis mean! O, whah's my po' chile gone; my po' baby!" exclaimed Mammy Judy, wringing her hands in distress.

"Stay, ole 'umin! De tree! De tree!" When, going out in the dark, feeling the trunk of the willow, three notches in the bark were distinct to the touch.

"Ole 'umin!" exclaimed Daddy Joe in a suppressed voice, hastening into the hut. "It am he, it am Henry got 'im!"

"Tang God, den my po' baby safe!" responded Mammy Judy, when they raised their voices in praise of thankfulness:

"O, who's like Jesus!
Hallelujah! praise ye the Lord;
O, who's like Jesus!
Hallelujah! love and serve the Lord!"

Falling upon their knees, the old man offered an earnest, heartful prayer to God, asking his guardianship through the night, and protection through the day, especially upon their heartbroken daughter, their runaway son-in-law, and the little grandson, when the two old people retired to rest with spirits mingled with joy, sorrow, hope, and fear; Ailcey going into the great house.

Chapter 11

A Shadow

"Ah, boys! Here you are, true to your promise," said Henry, as he entered a covert in the thicket adjacent the cotton place, late on Sunday evening, "have you been waiting long?"

"Not very," replied Andy, "not mo' dan two-three ouahs."

"I was fearful you would not come, or if you did before me, that you would grow weary, and leave."

"Yeh no call to doubt us Henry, case yeh fine us true as ole steel!"

"I know it," answered he, "but you know, Andy, that when a slave is once sold at auction, all respect for him—"

"O pshaw! we ain' goin' to heah nothin' like dat a tall! case—"

"No!" interrupted Charles, "all you got to do Henry, is to tell we boys what you want, an' we're your men."

"That's the talk for me!"

"Well, what you doin' here?" enquired Charles.

"W'at brought yeh back from Jackson so soon?" further enquired Andy.

"How did you get word to meet me here?"

"By Ailcey; she give me the stone, an' I give it to Andy, an' we both sent one apiece back. Didn't you git 'em?"

"Yes, that's the way I knew you intended to meet me," replied Henry.

"So we thought," said Charles, "but tell us, Henry, what you want us to do."

"I suppose you know all about the sale, that they had me on the auction block, but ordered a postponement, and—"

"That's the very pint we can't understand, although I'm in the same family with you," interrupted Charles.

"But tell us Henry, what yeh doin' here?" impatiently enquired Andy.

"Yes," added Charles, "we want to know."

"Well, I'm a runaway, and from this time forth, I swear—I do it religiously—that I'll never again serve any white man living!"

"That's the pint I wanted to git at before," explained Charles, "as I can't understan' why you run away, after your release from Jack Harris, an'—"

"Nah, I nuthah!" interrupted Andy.

"It seems to me," continued Charles, "that I'd 'ave went before they 'tempted to sell me, an' that you're safer now than before they had you on the block."

"Dat's da way I look at it," responded Andy.

"The stopping of the sale was to deceive his wife, mammy, and Daddy Joe, as he had privately disposed of me to a regular soul-driver by the name of Crow."

"I knows Dick Crow," said Andy, "'e come f'om Faginy, whah I did, da same town."

"So Ailcey said of him. Then you know him without any description from me," replied Henry.

"Yes 'n deed! an' I knows 'im to be a inhuman, mean, dead-po' white man, dat's wat I does."

"Well, I was privately sold to him for two thousand dollars, then ordered back to Franks, as though I was still his slave, and by him given a pass, and requested to go to Woodville where there were arrangements to seize me and hold me, till Crow ordered me, which was to have been on Tuesday evening. Crow is not aware of me having been given a pass; Franks gave it to deceive his wife, in case of my not returning, to make the impression that I had run away, when in reality I was sold to the trader."

"Then our people had their merrymaking all for nothin'," said Charles, "an' Franks got what 'e didn't deserve—their praise."

"No, the merrymaking was only to deceive Franks, that I might have time to get away. Daddy Joe, Mammy Judy, and Ailcey knew all about it, and proposed the feast to deceive him."

"Dat's good! Sarve 'im right, da 'sarned ole scamp!" rejoined Andy.

"It couldn't be better!" responded Charles.

"Henry uh wish we was in yo' place an' you none da wus by it," said Andy.

"Never mind, boys, give yourselves no uneasiness, as it wont be long before we'll all be together."

"You think so, Henry?" asked Charles.

"Well uh hope so, but den body can haudly 'spect it," responded Andy.

"Boys," said Henry, with great caution and much emotion, "I am now about to approach an important subject and as I have always found you true to me—and you can only be true to me by being true to yourselves—I shall not hesitate to impart it! But for Heaven's sake!—perhaps I had better not!"

"Keep nothin' back, Henry," said Charles, "as you know that we boys 'll die by our principles, that's settled!"

"Yes, I wants to die right now by mine; right heah, now!" sanctioned Andy.

"Well it is this—close, boys! close!" when they gathered in a huddle, beneath an underbush, upon their knees, "you both go with me, but not now. I—"

"Why not now?" anxiously enquired Charles.

"Dat's wat I like to know!" responded Andy.

"Stop, boys, till I explain. The plans are mine and you must allow me to know more about them than you. Just here, for once, the slave-holding preacher's advice to the black man is appropriate, 'Stand still and see the salvation.'"

"Then let us hear it, Henry," asked Charles.

"Fah God sake!" said Andy, "let us heah w'at it is, anyhow, Henry; yeh keep a body in 'spence so long, till I's mose crazy to heah it. Dat's no way!"

"You shall have it, but I approach it with caution! Nay, with fear and trembling, at the thought of what has been the fate of all previous matters of this kind. I approach it with religious fear, and hardly think us fit for the task; at least, I know I am not. But as no one has ever originated, or given us anything of the kind, I suppose I may venture."

"Tell it! tell it!" urged both in a whisper.

"Andy," said Henry, "let us have a word of prayer first!" when they bowed low, with their heads to the ground, Andy, who was a preacher of the Baptist pursuasion among his slave brethren, offering a solemn and affecting prayer, in whispers to the Most High, to give them knowledge and courage in the undertaking, and success in the effort.

Rising from their knees, Andy commenced an anthem, by which he appeared to be much affected, in the following words:

> *About our future destiny,*
> *There need be none debate—*
> *Whilst we ride on the tide,*
> *With our Captain and his mate.*

Clasping each other by the hand, standing in a band together, as a plight of their union and fidelity to each other, Henry said, "I now impart to you the secret, it is this: I have laid a scheme, and matured a plan for a general insurrection of the slaves in every state, and the successful overthrow of slavery!"

"Amen!" exclaimed Charles.

"God grant it!" responded Andy.

"Tell us, Henry, how's dis to be carried out?" enquired Andy.

"That's the thing which most concerns me, as it seems that it would be hard to do in the present ignorant state of our people in the slave States," replied Charles.

"Dat's jis wat I feah!" said Andy.

"This difficulty is obviated. It is so simple that the most stupid among the slaves will understand it as well as if he had been instructed for a year."

"What!" exclaimed Charles.

"Let's heah dat again!" asked Andy.

"It is so just as I told you! So simple is it that the trees of the forest or an orchard illustrate it; flocks of birds or domestic cattle, fields of corn, hemp, or sugar cane; tobacco, rice, or cotton, the whistling of the wind, rustling of the leaves, flashing of lightning, roaring of thunder, and running of streams all keep it constantly before their eyes and in their memory, so that they can't forget it if they would."

"Are we to know it now?" enquired Charles.

"I'm boun' to know it dis night befo' I goes home, 'case I been longin' fah ole Pottah dis many day, an' uh mos' think uh got 'im now!"

"Yes boys, you've to know it before we part, but—"

"That's the talk!" said Charles.

"Good nuff talk fah me!" responded Andy.

"As I was about to say, such is the character of this organization, that punishment and misery are made the instruments for its propagation, so—"

"I can't understan' that part—"

"You know nothing at all about it Charles, and you must—"

"Stan' still an' see da salvation!" interrupted Andy.

"Amen!" responded Charles.

"God help you so to do, brethren!" admonished Henry.

"Go on Henry tell us! give it to us!" they urged.

"Every blow you receive from the oppressor impresses the organization upon your mind, making it so clear that even Whitehead's Jack could understand it as well as his master."

"We are satisfied! The secret, the secret!" they importuned.

"Well then, first to prayer, and then to the organization. Andy!" said Henry, nodding to him, when they again bowed low with their heads to the ground, whilst each breathed a silent prayer, which was ended with "Amen" by Andy.

Whilst yet upon their knees, Henry imparted to them the secrets of his organization.

"O, dat's da thing!" exclaimed Andy.

"Capital, capital!" responded Charles. "What fools we was that we didn't know it long ago!"

"I is mad wid myse'f now!" said Andy.

"Well, well, well! Surely God must be in the work," continued Charles.

"'E's heah; Heaven's nigh! Ah feels it! It's right heah!" responded Andy, placing his hand upon his chest, the tears trickling down his cheeks.

"Brethren," asked Henry, "do you understand it?"

"Understand it? Why, a child could understand, it's so easy!" replied Charles.

"Yes," added Andy, "ah not only undestan' myse'f, but wid da knowledge I has uv it, ah could make Whitehead's Jack a Moses!"

"Stand still, then, and see!" said he.

"Dat's good Bible talk!" responded Andy.

"Well, what is we to do?" enquired Charles.

"You must now go on and organize continually. It makes no difference when, nor where you are, so that the slaves are true and trustworthy, as the scheme is adapted to all times and places."

"How we gwine do Henry, 'bout gittin' da things 'mong da boys?" enquired Andy.

"All you have to do, is to find one good man or woman—I don't care which, so that they prove to be the right person—on a single plantation, and hold a seclusion and impart the secret to them, and make them the organizers for their own plantation, and they in like manner impart it to some other next to them, and so on. In this way it will spread like smallpox among them."

"Henry, you is fit fah leadah ah see," complimentingly said Andy.

"I greatly mistrust myself, brethren, but if I can't command, I can at least plan."

"Is they anything else for us to do Henry?" enquired Charles.

"Yes, a very important part of your duties has yet to be stated. I now go as a runaway, and will be suspected of lurking about in the thickets, swamps and caves; then to make the ruse complete, just as often as you think it necessary, to make a good impression, you must kill a shoat, take a lamb, pig, turkey, goose, chickens, ham of bacon from the smoke house, a loaf of bread or crock of butter from the spring house, and throw them down into the old waste well at the back of the old quarters, always leaving the heads of the fowls lying about and the blood of the larger animals. Everything that is missed dont hesitate to lay it upon me, as a runaway, it will only cause them to have the less suspicion of your having such a design."

"That's it—the very thing!" said Charles. "An it so happens that they's an ole waste well on both Franks' and Potter's places, one for both of us."

"I hope Andy, you have no religious objections to this?"

"It's a paut ah my 'ligion Henry, to do whateveh I bleve right, an' shall sholy do dis, God being my helpah!"

"Now he's talkin!" said Charles.

"You must make your religion subserve your interests, as your oppressors do theirs!" advised Henry. "They use the Scriptures to make you submit, by preaching to you the texts of 'obedience to your masters' and 'standing still to see the salavation,' and we must now begin to understand the Bible so as to make it of interest to us."

"Dat's gospel talk," sanctioned Andy. "Is da anything else yeh want tell us boss—I calls 'im boss, 'case 'e aint nothing else but 'boss'—so we can make 'ase an' git to wuck? 'case I feels like goin' at 'em now, me!"

"Having accomplished our object, I think I have done, and must leave you tomorrow."

"When shall we hear from you, Henry?" enquired Charles.

"Not until you shall see me again; when that will be, I don't know. You may see me in six months, and might not not in eighteen. I am determined, now that I am driven to it, to complete an organization in every slave state before I return, and have fixed two years as my utmost limit."

"Henry, tell me before we part, do you know anything about little Joe?" enquired Charles.

"I do!"

"Wha's da chile?" enquired Andy.

"He's safe enough, on his way to Canada!" at which Charles and Andy laughed.

"Little Joe is on 'is way to Canada?" said Andy. "Mighty young travelah!"

"Yes," replied Henry with a smile.

"You're a-joking Henry?" said Charles, enquiringly.

"I am serious, brethren," replied he. "I do not joke in matters of this kind. I smiled because of Andy's surprise."

"How did 'e go?" further enquired Andy.

"In company with his 'mother' who was waiting on her 'mistress!'" replied he quaintly.

"Eh heh!" exclaimed Andy. "I knows all 'bout it now; but whah'd da 'mammy' come from?"

"I found one!"

"Aint 'e high!" said Andy.

"Well, brethren, my time is drawing to a close," said Henry, rising to his feet.

"O!" exclaimed Andy. "Ah like to forgot, has yeh any money Henry?"

"Have either of you any?"

"We has."

"How much?"

"I got two-three hundred dollahs!" replied Andy.

"An' so has I, Henry!" added Charles.

"Then keep it, as I have two thousand dollars now around my waist, and you'll find use for all you've got, and more, as you will before long have an opportunity of testing. Keep this studiously in mind and impress it as an important part of the scheme of organization, that they must have money, if they want to get free. Money will obtain them everything necessary by which to obtain their liberty. The money is within all of their reach if they only knew it was right to take it. God told the Egyptian slaves to 'borrow from their neighbors'—meaning their oppressors—'all their jewels;' meaning to take their money and wealth wherever they could lay hands upon it, and depart from Egypt. So you must teach them to take all the money they can get from their masters, to enable them to make the strike without a failure. I'll show you when we leave for the North, what money will do for you, right here in Mississippi. Bear this in mind; it is your certain passport through the white gap, as I term it."

"I means to take all ah can git; I bin doin' dat dis some time. Ev'ry time ole Pottah leave 'is money pus, I borrys some, an' e' all'as lays it on Miss Mary, but 'e think so much uh huh, dat anything she do is right wid 'im. Ef 'e 'spected me, an' Miss Mary say 'twant me, dat would be 'nough fah 'im."

"That's right!" said Henry. "I see you have been putting your own interpretation on the Scriptures, Andy, and as Charles will now have to take my place, he'll have still a much better opportunity than you, to 'borrow from his master.'"

"You needn't fear, I'll make good use of my time!" replied Charles.

The slaves now fell upon their knees in silent communion, all being affected to the shedding of tears, a period being put to their devotion by a sorrowful trembling of Henry's voice singing to the following touching words:

> *Farewell, farewell, farewell!*
> *My loving friends farewell!*
> *Farewell old comrades in the cause,*
> *I leave you here, and journey on;*
> *And if I never more return,*
> *Farewell, I'm bound to meet you there!*

"One word before we part," said Charles. "If we never should see you again, I suppose you intend to push on this scheme?"

"Yes!"

> *"Insurrection shall be my theme!*
> *My watchword 'Freedom or the grave!'*
> *Until from Rappahannock's stream,*
> *To where the Cuato waters lave,*
> *One simultaneous war cry*
> *Shall burst upon the midnight air!*
> *And rouse the tyrant but to sigh—*
> *Mid sadness, wailing, and despair!"*

Grasping each eagerly by the hand, the tears gushing from his eyes, with an humble bow, he bid them finally "farewell!" and the runaway was off through the forest.

Chapter 12

The Discovery

I t can't be; I won't believe it!" said Franks at the breakfast table on Sunday morning, after hearing that little Joe was missed. "He certainly must be lost in the shrubbery."

After breakfast a thorough search was made, none being more industrious than Ailcey in hunting the little fugitive, but without success.

"When was he last seen?" enquired Franks.

"He wah put to bed las' night while we wuh at de suppeh seh!" replied Ailcey.

"There's something wrong about this thing, Mrs. Franks, and I'll be hanged if I don't ferret out the whole before I'm done with it!" said the Colonel.

"I hope you don't suspect me as—"

"Nonsense! my dear, not at all—nothing of the sort, but I do suspect respectable parties in another direction."

"Gracious, Colonel! Whom have you reference to? I'm sure I can't imagine."

"Well, well, we shall see! Ailcey, call Judy."

"Maus Stephen, yeh sen' fah me?" enquired the old woman, puffing and blowing.

"Yes, Judy. Do you know anything about little Joe? I want you to tell me the truth!" sternly enquired Franks.

"Maus Stephen! I cah lie! so long as yeh had me, yu nah missus neveh knows me tell lie. No, bless de Laud! Ah sen' my soul to de ole boy dat way? No maus Stephen, ah uhdn give wat I feels in my soul—"

"Well never mind, Judy, about your soul, but tell us about—"

"Ah! maus Stephen, ah 'spects to shout wen de wul's on fiah! an—"

"Tell us about the boy, Judy, and we'll hear about your religion another time."

"If you give her a little time, Colonel, I think she'll be able to tell about him!" suggested Mrs. Franks on seeing the old woman weeping.

"Sho, mammy!" said Ailcey in a whisper with a nudge, standing behind her, "wat yeh stan' heah cryin' befo' dese ole wite folks fah!"

"Come, come, Judy! what are you crying about! let us hear quickly what you've got to say. Don't be frightened!"

"No maus Stephen, I's not feahed; ah could run tru troop a hosses an' face de debil! My soul's happy, my soul's on fiah! Whoo! Blessed Jesus! Ride on, King!" when the old woman tossed and tumbled about so dexterously, that the master and mistress considered themselves lucky in getting out of the way.

"The old thing's crazy! We'll not be able to get anything out of her, Mrs. Franks."

"No maus Stephen, blessed be God a'mighty! I's not crazy, but sobeh as a judge! An—"

"Then let us hear about little Joe, as you can understand so well what is said around you, and let us have no more of your whooping and nonsense, distracting the neighborhood!"

"Blessed God! Blessed God! Laud sen' a nudah gale! O, fah a nudah showeh!"

"I really believe she's crazy! We've now been here over an hour, and no nearer the information than before."

"I think she's better now!" said Mrs. Franks.

"Judy, can you compose yourself long enough to answer my questions?" enquired Franks.

"O yes, mausta! ah knows wat I's 'bout, but w'en mausta Jesus calls, ebry body mus' stan' back, case 'e's 'bove all!"

"That's all right, Judy, all right; but let us hear about little Joe—do you know anything about him, where he is, or how he was taken away?"

"'E wah dah Sattiday night, maus Stephen."

"What time, Judy, on Saturday evening was he there?"

"W'en da wah eatin suppeh, seh."

"How do you know, when you were at the lower quarters, and he in your hut?"

"'E wah put to bed den."

"Who put him to bed—you?"

"No, seh, Ailcey."

"Ailcey—who went with her, any one?"

"Yes seh, Van Wintah Ben went wid uh."

"Van Winter's Ben! I thought we'd get at the thieves presently; I knew I'd ferret it out! Well now, Judy, I ask you as a Christian, and expect you to act with me as one Christian with another—has not Mrs. Van Winter been talking to you about this boy?"

"No seh, nebeh!"

"Nor to Henry?"

"No seh!"

"Did not she, to your knowledge, send Ben there that night to steal away little Joe?"

"No, seh!"

"Did you not hear Ailcey tell some one, or talking in her sleep, say that Mrs. Van Winter had something to do with the abduction of that boy?"

"Maus Stephen, ah do'n undehstan' dat duckin uh duckshun, dat w'at yeh call it—dat big wud!"

"O! 'abduction' means stealing away a person, Judy."

"Case ah waun gwine tell nothin 'bout it."

"Well, what do you know, Judy?"

"As dah's wud a troof in me, ah knows nothin' 'bout it."

"Well, Judy, you can go now. She's an honest old creature, I believe!" said Franks, as the old fat cook turned away.

"Yes, poor old black fat thing! She's religious to a fault," replied Mrs. Franks.

"Well, Ailcey, what do you know about it?" enquired the master.

"Nothin' seh, o'ny Mammy Judy ask me toat 'im up to da hut an' put 'im in bed."

"Well, did you do it?"

"Yes, seh!"

"Did Ben go with you?"

"Yes, seh!"

"Did he return with you to the lower quarters?"

"Yes, seh!"

"Did he not go back again, or did he remain in the house?"

"'E stay in."

"Did you not see some one lurking about the house when you took the boy up to the hut?"

"Ah tot ah heahn some un in da bushes, but Ben say 'twan no one."

"Now Ailcey, don't you know who that was?"

"No, seh!"

"Was'nt it old Joe?"

"No, seh, lef' 'im in de low quahteh."

"Was it Henry?"

"Dun no, seh!"

"Wasn't it Mrs. Van Winter's—"

"Why Colonel!" exclaimed Mrs. Franks with surprise.

"Negroes, I mean! You didn't let me finish the sentence, my dear!" explained he, correcting his error.

"Ah dun'o, seh!"

"Now tell me candidly, my girl, who and what you thought it was at the time?"

"Ah do'n like to tell!" replied the girl, looking down.

"Tell, Ailcey! Who do you think it was, and what they were after?" enquired Mrs. Franks.

"Ah do'n waun tell, missus!"

"Tell, you goose you! did you see any one?" continued Franks.

"Ah jis glance 'em."

"Was the person close to you?" further enquired Mrs. Franks.

"Yes, um, da toched me on da shouldeh an' run."

"Well, why don't you tell then, Ailcey, who you thought it was, and what they were after, you stubborn jade you, speak!" stormed Franks, stamping his foot.

"Don't get out of temper, Colonel! make some allowance for her under the circumstances. Now tell, Ailcey, what you thought at the time?" mildly asked Mrs. Franks.

"Ah tho't t'wah maus Stephen afteh me."

"Well, if you know nothing about it, you may go now!" gruffly replied her master. "These Negroes are not to be trusted. They will endeavor to screen each other if they have the least chance to do so. I'll sell that girl!"

"Colonel, don't be hasty in this matter, I beg of you!" said Mrs. Franks earnestly.

"I mean to let her go to the man she most hates, that's Crow."

"Why do you think she hates Crow so badly?"

"By the side looks she gives him when he comes into the house."

"I pray you then, Colonel, to attempt no more auction sales, and you may avoid unpleasant association in that direction."

"Yes, by the by, speaking of the auction, I really believe Mrs. Van Winter had something to do with the abduction of that little Negro."

"I think you do her wrong, Colonel Franks; she's our friend, and aside from this, I don't think her capable of such a thing."

"Such friendship is worse than open enmity, my dear, and should be studiously shunned."

"I must acquit her, Colonel, of all agency in this matter."

"Well, mark what I tell you, Mrs. Franks, you'll yet hear more of it, and that too at no distant day."

"Well it may be, but I can't think so."

"'May be'! I'm sure so. And more: I believe that boy has been induced to take advantage of my clemency, and run away. I'll make an example of him, because what one Negro succeeds in doing, another will attempt. I'll have him at any cost. Let him go on this way and there won't be a Negro in the neighborhood presently."

"Whom do you mean, Colonel?"

"I mean that ingrate Henry, that's who."

"Henry gone!"

"I have no doubt of it at all, as he had a pass to Woodville and Jackson; and now that the boy is stolen by someone, I've no doubt himself. I might have had some leniency towards him had he not committed a theft, a crime of all others the most detestable in my estimation."

"And Henry is really gone?" with surprise again enquired Mrs. Franks.

"He is, my dear, and you appear to be quite inquisitive about it!" remarked Franks as he thought he observed a concealed smile upon her lips.

"I am inquisitive, Colonel, because whatever interests you should interest me."

"By Monday evening, hanged if I don't know all about this thing. Ailcey, call Charles to get my saddle horse!"

"Charles ain' heah, maus Stephen."

"Where's old Joe?"

"At de hut, seh."

"Tell him to saddle Oscar immediately, and bring him to the door."

"Yes, seh!" replied the girl, lightly tripping away.

The horse was soon at the door, and with his rider cantering away.

"Tony, what is Mammy Judy about?" enquired Mrs. Franks as evening approached.

"She's sif'en meal, missus, to make mush fah ouah suppah."

"You must tell mammy not to forget me, Tony, in the distribution of her mush and milk."

"Yes, missus, ah tell uh right now!" when away ran Tony bearing the message, eager as are all children to be the agents of an act of kindness.

Mammy Judy, smiling, received the message with the assurance of "Yes, dat she shall hab much as she want!" when, turning about, she gave

MARTIN R. DELANY

strict orders that Ailcey neglect not to have a china bowl in readiness to receive the first installment of the hasty pudding.

The hut of Mammy Judy served as a sort of headquarters on Saturday and Sunday evenings for the slaves from the plantation, and those in town belonging to the "estate," who this evening enjoyed a hearty laugh at the expense of Daddy Joe.

Slaves are not generally supplied with light in their huts; consequently, except from the fat of their meat and that gathered about the kitchen with which they make a "lamp," and the use of pinewood tapers, they eat and do everything about their dwellings in the dark.

Hasty pudding for the evening being the bill of fare, all sat patiently awaiting the summon of Mammy Judy, some on blocks, some on logs of wood, some on slab benches, some on inverted buckets and half-barrel wash tubs, and whatever was convenient, while many of the girls and other young people were seated on the floor around against the wall.

"Hush, chilen!" admonished Mammy Judy, after carefully seeing that each one down to Tony had been served with a quota from the kettle.

"Laud, make us truly tankful fah wat we 'bout to 'ceive!" petitioned Daddy Joe with uplifted hands. "Top dah wid yo' nause an' nonsense ole people cah heah deh yeahs to eat!" admonished the old man as he took the pewter dish between his knees and commenced an earnest discussion of its contents. "Do'n yeh heah me say hush dah? Do'n yeh heah!"

"Joe!" was the authoritative voice from without.

"Sah!"

"Take my horse to the stable!"

"Yes, sah!" responded the old man, sitting down his bowl of mush and milk on the hearth in the corner of the jam. "Do'n any on yeh toch dat, yeh heah?"

"We ain gwine to, Daddy Joe," replied the young people.

"Huccum de young folks, gwine eat yo' mush and milk? Sho, ole man, g'long whah yeh gwine, ad' let young folk 'lone!" retorted Mammy Judy.

On returning from the stable, in his hurry the old man took up the bowl of a young man who sat it on his stool for the moment.

"Yoheh, Daddy Joe, dat my mush!" said the young man.

"Huccum dis yone?" replied the old man.

"Wy, ah put it dah; yeh put yone in de chimbly connoh."

"Ah! Dat eh did!" exclaimed he, taking up the bowl eating heartily. "Wat dat yeh all been doin' heah? Some on yeh young folks been prankin' long wid dis mush an' milk!" continued the old man, champing and chewing in a manner which indicated something more solid than mush and milk.

"Deed we did'n, Daddy Joe; did'n do nothin' to yo' mush an' milk, so we did'n!" replied Ailcey, whose word was always sufficient with the old people.

"Hi, what dis in heah! Sumpen mighty crisp!" said Daddy Joe, still eating heartily and now and again blowing something from his mouth like coarse meal husks. "Sumpen heah mighty crisp, ah tells yeh! Ole umin, light dat pine knot dah; so dahk yeh cah'n see to talk. Git light dah quick ole umin! Sumpen heah mighty crisp in dis mush an' milk!— Mighty crisp!"

"Good Laud! see dah now! Ah tole yeh so!" exclaimed Mammy Judy when, on producing a light, the bowl was found to be partially filled with large black house roaches.

"Reckon Daddy Joe do'n tank'im fah dat!" said little Tony, referring to the blessing of the old man; amidst an outburst of tittering and snickering among the young people.

Daddy Joe lost his supper, when the slaves retired for the evening.

Chapter 13

Perplexity

Early on Monday morning Colonel Franks arose to start for Woodville and Jackson in search of the fugitive.

"My dear, is Ailcey up? Please call Tony," said Mrs. Franks, the boy soon appearing before his mistress. "Tony, call Ailcey," continued she, "your master is up and going to the country."

"Missus Ailcey ain' dah!" replied the boy, returning in haste from the nursery.

"Certainly she is; did you go into the nursery?"

"Yes, um!"

"Are the children there?"

"Yes, um, boph on 'em."

"Then she can't be far—she'll be in presently."

"Missus, she ain' come yit," repeated the boy after a short absence.

"Did you look in the nursery again?"

"Yes, um!"

"Are the children still in bed?"

"Yes, um, boph sleep, only maus George awake."

"You mean one asleep and the other awake!" said Mrs. Franks, smiling.

"Yes um boph wake!" replied the boy.

"Didn't you tell me, Tony, that your master George only was awake?" asked the mistress.

"Miss Matha sleep fus, den she wake up and talk to maus George," explained the boy, his master laughing, declared that a Negro's skull was too thick to comprehend anything.

"Don't mistake yourself, Colonel!" replied Mrs. Franks. "That boy is anything but a blockhead, mind that!"

"My dear, can't you see something about that girl?" said the Colonel.

"Run quickly, Tony, and see if Ailcey is in the hut," bade Mrs. Franks.

"Dear me," continued she, "since the missing of little Joe, she's all gossip, and we needn't expect much of her until the thing has died away."

"She'll not gossip after today, my dear!" replied the Colonel decisively, "as I'm determined to put her in my pocket in time, before she is decoyed away by that ungrateful wretch, who is doubtless ready for anything, however vile, for revenge."

Ailcey was a handsome black girl, graceful and intelligent, but having been raised on the place, had not the opportunity of a house maid for refinement. The Colonel, having had a favorable opinion of her as a servant, frequently requested that she be taken from the field, long before it had been done. This had not the most favorable impression upon the mind of his lady, who since the morning of the interview, the day before, had completely turned against the girl.

Mrs. Franks was an amiable lady and lenient mistress, but did a slave offend, she might be expected to act as a mistress; and still more, she was a woman; but concerning Ailcey she was mistaken, as a better and more pure-hearted female slave there was not to be found; and as true to her mistress and her honor, as was Maggie herself.

"Missus, she ain't dare nudder! aun' Judy ain seed 'er from las' night!" said the boy who came running up the stairs.

"Then call Charles immediately!" ordered she; when away went he and shortly came Charles.

"Servant, mist'ess!" saluted Charles, as he entered her presence.

"Charles, do you know anything of Ailcey?" enquired she.

"No mist'ess I don't."

"When did you see her last?"

"Last night, ma'm."

"Was she in company with anyone?"

"Yes ma'm, Potter's Rachel."

"What time in the evening was it, Charles?"

"After seven o'clock, ma'm."

"O, she was home after that and went to bed in the nursery, where she has been sleeping for several nights."

"My dear, this thing must be probed to the bottom at once! things are taking such a strange course, that we don't know whom to trust. I'll be hanged if I understand it!" The carriage being ordered, they went directly down to 'squire Potter's.

"Good morning Mrs. Potter!—you will pardon us for the intrusion at so early an hour, but as the errand may concern us all, I'll not stop to be ceremonious—do I find the 'squire in?"

The answer being in the affirmative, a servant being in attendance, the old gentleman soon made his appearance.

"Good morning, Colonel and Madam Franks!" saluted he.

"Good morning, 'squire! I shan't be ceremonious, and to give you a history of my errand, and to make a short story of a long one, we'll 'make a lump job of it,' to use a homely phrase."

"I know the 'squire will be interested!" added Mrs. Franks.

"No doubt of it at all, ma'm!" replied Mrs. Potter, who seemed to anticipate them.

"It is this," resumed the Colonel. "On Friday I gave my boy Henry verbal permission to go to the country, when he pretended to leave. On Saturday evening during the Negro-gathering at the old quarters, my little Negro boy Joe was stolen away, and on last evening, our Negro girl Ailcey the nurse, cleared out, and it seems was last seen in company with your Negro girl Rachel."

"Titus, call Rachel there! No doubt but white men are at the bottom of it," said Potter.

"Missus, heah I is!" drawled the girl awkwardly, with a curtsy.

"Speak to your master there; he wants you," ordered Mrs. Potter.

"Mausta!" saluted the girl.

"Rachel, my girl, I want you to tell me, were you with Colonel Franks' black girl Ailcey on last evening?"

"Yes seh, I wah."

"Where, Rachel?" continued the master.

"Heah seh, at ouah house."

"Where did you go to?"

"We go down to docteh Denny."

"What for—what took you down to Dr. Denny's, Rachel?"

"Went 'long wid Ailcey."

"What did Ailcey go there for—do you know?"

"Went dah to see Craig' Polly."

"Craig's Polly, which of Mr. Craig's Negro girls is that?"

"Dat un w'ot mos' white."

"Well, was Polly there?"

"She waun dah w'en we go, but she soon come."

"Why did you go to Dr. Denny's to meet Polly?"

"Ailcey say Polly go'n to meet uh dah."

"Well, did they leave there when you did?"

"Yes, seh."

"Where did you go to then?"

"I come home, seh."

"Where did they go?"

"Da say da go'n down undah da Hill."

"Who else was with them besides you?"

"No un, seh."

"Was there no man with them, when they left for under the Hill?"

"No, seh."

"Did you see no man about at all, Rachel?"

"No, seh."

"Now don't be afraid to tell: was there no white person at all spoke to you when together last night?"

"None but some white gent'men come up an' want walk wid us, same like da al'as do we black girls w'en we go out."

"Did the girls seem to be acquainted and glad to see them?"

"No seh, the girls run, and da gent'men cus—"

"Never mind that, Rachel, you can go now," concluded her master.

"Well, 'squire, hanged if this thing mus'nt be stopped! Four slaves in less than that many days gone from under our very eyes, and we unable to detect them! It's insufferable, and I believe whites to be at the head of it! I have my suspicions on a party who stands high in the community, and—"

"Now Colonel, if you please!" interrupted Mrs. Franks.

"Well, I suppose we'll have for the present to pass that by," replied he.

"Indeed, something really should be done!" said the 'squire.

"Yes, and that quickly, if we would keep our Negroes to prevent us from starving."

"I THINK THE THING SHOULD at once be seen into; what say you, Colonel?"

"As I have several miles to ride this morning," said Franks, looking at his watch, it now being past nine o'clock, "I must leave so as to be back in the evening. Any steps that may be taken before my return, you have the free use of my name. Good morning!"

A few minutes and the Colonel was at his own door, astride of a horse, and on his way to Woodville.

Chapter 14

GAD AND GOSSIP

This day the hut of Mammy Judy seemed to be the licensed resort for all the slaves of the town; and even many whites were seen occasionally to drop in and out, as they passed along. Everyone knew the residence of Colonel Franks, and many of the dusky inhabitants of the place were solely indebted to the purse-proud occupants of the "great house" for their introduction to that part of Mississippi.

For years he and Major Armsted were the only reliable traders upon whom could be depended for a choice gang of field Negroes and other marketable people. And not only this section, but the whole Mississippi Valley to some extent was to them indebted. First as young men the agents of Woolford, in maturer age their names became as household words and known as the great proprietary Mississippi or Georgia Negro-traders.

Domestic service seemed for the time suspended, and little required at home to do, as the day was spent as a kind of gala-day, in going about from place to place talking of everything.

Among the foremost of these was Mammy Judy, for although she partially did, and was expected to stay and be at home today, and act as an oracle, yet she merely stole a little time to run over to Mrs. Van Winter's, step in at 'squire Potter's to speak a word to Milly, drop by Dr. Denny's, and just poke in her head at Craig's a moment.

"Ah been tellin' on 'em so! All along ah been tellin' on 'em, but da uden bleve me!" soliloquized Mammy Judy, when the first dash of news through the boy Tony reached her, that Ailcey had gone and taken with her some of 'squire Potter's people, several of Dr. Denny's, a gang of Craig's, and half of Van Winter's. "Dat jis wat ah been tellin' on 'em all along, but da uden bleve me!" concluded she.

"Yeah heah de news!" exclaimed Potter's Minney to Van Winter's Biddy.

"I heah dat Ailcey gone!" replied Biddy.

"Dat all; no mo?" enquired the girl with a high turban of Madras on her head.

"I heahn little Joe go too!"

"Didn yeh heah dot Denny' Sookey, an' Craig' Polly, took a whole heap uh Potteh' people an' clah'd out wid two po' white mens, an' dat da all seen comin' out Van Winteh de old ablish'neh, soon in de monin' fo' day?"

"No!" replied the good-natured, simple-hearted Biddy, "I did'n!"

"Yes, sho's yeh baun dat true, case uhly dis monin' cunel Frank' an' lady come see mausta—and yeh know 'e squiah an' make de law—an' mauster ghin 'em papehs, an' da go arter de Judge to put heh in jail!"

"Take who to jail?"

"Wy, dat ole ablish'neh, Miss Van Winteh! Ah wish da all dead, dese ole ablish'nehs, case da steal us an' sell us down souph to haud maustas, w'en we got good places. Any how she go'n to jail, an' I's glad!"

Looking seriously at her, Biddy gave a long sigh, saying nothing to commit herself, but going home, communicated directly to her mistress that which she heard, as Mrs. Van Winter was by all regarded as a friend to the Negro race, and at that time the subject of strong suspicion among the slaveholders of the neighborhood.

Eager to gad and gossip, from place to place the girl Minney passed about relating the same to each and all with whom she chanced to converse, they imparting to others the same strange story, until reaching the ears of intelligent whites who had heard no other version, it spread through the city as a statement of fact.

Learning as many did by sending to the house, that the Colonel that day had gone in search of his slaves, the statement was confirmed as having come from Mrs. Franks, who was known to be a firm friend of Mrs. Van Winter.

"Upon my word!" said Captain Grason on meeting Sheriff Hughes. "Sheriff, things are coming to a pretty pass!"

"What's that, Captain?" enquired the Sheriff.

"Have you not heard the news yet, concerning the Negroes?"

"Why, no! I've been away to Vicksburg the last ten days, and just getting back."

"O, Heavens! we're no longer safe in our own houses. Why, sir, we're about being overwhelmed by an infamous class of persons who live in our midst, and eat at our tables!"

"You surprise me, Captain! what's the matter?"

"Sir, it would take a week to relate the particulars, but our slaves are running off by wholesale. On Sunday night a parcel of Colonel Franks' Negroes left, a lot of Dr. Denny's, some of 'squire Potter's, and a gang of Craig's, aided by white men, whom together with the Negroes were seen before day in the morning coming out of the widow Van Winters, who was afterwards arrested, and since taken before the judge on a writ of habeas corpus, but the circumstances against her being so strong she was remanded for trial, which so far strengthens the accusation. I know not where this thing will end!"

"Surprising indeed, sir!" replied Hughes. "I had not heard of it before, but shall immediately repair to her house, and learn all the facts in the case. I am well acquainted with Mrs. Van Winter—in fact she is a relation of my wife—and must hasten. Good day, sir!"

On ringing the bell, a quick step brought a person to the door, when on being opened, the Sheriff found himself in the warm embraces of the kind-hearted and affectionate Mrs. Van Winter herself.

After the usual civilities, she was the first to introduce the subject, informing him of their loss by their mutual friends Colonel Franks and lady, with others, and no surprise was greater than that on hearing the story current concerning herself.

Mammy Judy was as busy as she well could be, in hearing and telling news among the slaves who continually came and went through the day. So overwhelmed with excitement was she, that she had little else to say in making a period, then "All a long ah been tellin' on yeh so, but yeh uden bleve me!"

Among the many who thronged the hut was Potter's Milly. She in person is black, stout and fat, bearing a striking resemblance to the matronly old occupant Mammy Judy. For two hours or more letting a number come in, gossip, and pass out, only to be immediately succeeded by another; who like the old country woman who for the first time in visiting London all day stood upon the sidewalk of the principal thoroughfare waiting till the crowd of people and cavalcade of vehicles passed, before she made the attempt to cross the street; she sat waiting till a moment would occur by which in private to impart a secret to her friend alone. That moment did at last arrive.

"Judy!" said the old woman in a whisper. "Ah been waitin' all day long to see yeh fah sumpen' ticlar!"

"W'at dat, Milly?" whispered Mammy Judy scarcely above her breath.

"I's gwine too!" and she hurried away to prepare supper for the white folks, before they missed her, though she had been absent full two hours and a half, another thirty minutes being required for the fat old woman to reach the house.

"Heah dat now!" whispered Mammy Judy. "Ah tole yeh so!"

"Well, my dear, not a word of that graceless dog, the little Negro, nor that girl," said Franks who had just returned from the country, "but I am fully compensated for the disappointment, on learning of the arrest and imprisonment of that—!"

"Who, Colonel?" interrupted his wife.

"I hope after this you'll be willing to set some estimation on my judgment—I mean your friend Mrs. Van Winter the abolitionist!"

"I beg your pardon, Colonel, as nothing is farther from the truth! From whom did you receive that intelligence?"

"I met Captain Grason on his way to Woodville, who informed me that it was current in town, and you had corroborated the statement. Did you see him?"

"Nothing of the kind, sir, and it has not been more than half an hour since Mrs. Van Winter left here, who heartily sympathizes with us, though she has her strange notions that black people have as much right to freedom as white."

"Well, my dear, we'll drop the subject!" concluded the Colonel with much apparent disappointment.

The leading gentlemen of the town and neighborhood assembled inaugurating the strictest vigilant police regulations, when after free and frequent potations of brandy and water, of which there was no scarcity about the Colonel's mansion, the company separated, being much higher spirited, if not better satisfied, than when they met in council.

This evening Charles and Andy met each other in the street, but in consequence of the strict injunction on the slaves by the patrol law recently instituted, they only made signs as they passed, intending to meet at a designated point. But the patrol reconnoitred so closely in their track, they were driven entirely from their purpose, retiring to their homes for the night.

Chapter 15

Interchange of Opinion

The landing of a steamer on her downward trip brought Judge Ballard and Major Armsted to Natchez. The Judge had come to examine the country, purchase a cotton farm, and complete the arrangements of an interest in the "Merchantman." Already the proprietor of a large estate in Cuba, he was desirous of possessing a Mississippi cotton place. Disappointed by the absence of his wife abroad, he was satisfied to know that her object was accomplished.

Major Armsted was a man of ripe intelligence, acquired by years of rigid experience and close observation, rather than literary culture, though his educational attainments as a business man were quite respectable. He for years had been the partner in business with Colonel Stephen Franks. In Baltimore, Washington City, Annapolis, Richmond, Norfolk, Charlestown, and Winchester, Virginia, a prison or receptacle for coffle-gangs of slaves purchased and sold in the market, comprised their principal places of business in the slaveowning states of the Union.

The Major was a great jester, full of humor, and fond of a good joke, ever ready to give and take such even from a slave. A great common sense man, by strict attention to men and things, and general observation, had become a philosopher among his fellows.

"Quite happy to meet you, Judge, in these parts!" greeted Franks. "Wonder you could find your way so far south, especially at such a period, these being election times!"

"Don't matter a bit, as he's not up for anything I believe just now, except for Negro-trading! And in that he is quite a proselyte, and heretic to the teachings of his Northern faith!" jocosely remarked Armsted.

"Don't mistake me, gentlemen, because it was the incident of my life to be born in a nonslaveholding state. I'm certain that I am not at all understood as I should be on this question!" earnestly replied the Judge.

"The North has given you a bad name, Judge, and it's difficult to separate yourself now from it, holding the position that you do, as one of her ablest jurists," said Armsted.

"Well, gentlemen!" seriously replied the Judge. "As regards my opinion of Negro slavery, the circumstances which brought me here, my large interest and responsibility in the slave-labor products of Cuba, should be, I think, sufficient evidence of my fidelity to Southern principles, to say nothing of my official records, which modesty should forbid my reference to."

"Certainly, certainly, Judge! The Colonel is at fault. He has lost sight of the fact that you it was who seized the first runaway Negro by the throat and held him by the compromise grasp until we Southern gentlemen sent for him and had him brought back!"

"Good, good, by hookie!" replied the Colonel, rubbing his hands together.

"I hope I'm understood, gentlemen!" seriously remarked the Judge.

"I think so, Judge, I think so!" replied Armsted, evidently designing a full commitment on the part of the Judge. "And if not, a little explanation will set us right."

"It is true that I have not before been engaged in the slave trade, because until recently I had conscientious scruples about the thing—and I suppose I'm allowed the right of conscience as well as other folks," smilingly said the Judge, "never having purchased but for peopling my own plantation. But a little sober reflection set me right on that point. It is plain that the right to buy implies the right to hold, also to sell; and if there be right in the one, there is in the other; the premise being right, the conclusion follows as a matter of course. I have therefore determined, not only to buy and hold, but buy and sell also. As I have heretofore been interested for the trade I will become interested in it."

"Capital, capital, by George! That's conclusive. Charles! A pitcher of cool water here; Judge, take another glass of brandy."

"Good, very good!" said Armsted. "So far, but there is such a thing as feeding out of two cribs—present company, you know, and so—ahem!—therefore we should like to hear the Judge's opinion of equality, what it means anyhow. I'm anxious to learn some of the doctrines of human rights, not knowing how soon I may be called upon to practice them, as I may yet marry some little Yankee girl, full of her Puritan notions. And I'm told an old bachelor 'can't come it' up that way, except he has a 'pocket full of rocks,' and can talk philanthropy like old Wilberforce."

"Here, gentlemen, I beg to make an episode, before replying to Major Armsted," suggested the Judge. "His jest concerning the Yankee girl reminds me—and I hope it may not be amiss in saying so—that my lady is the daughter of a clergyman, brought up amidst the sand of New

England, and I think I'll not have to go from the present company to prove her a good slaveholder. So the Major may see that we northerners are not all alike."

"How about the Compromise measures, Judge? Stand up to the thing all through, and no flinching."

"My opinion, sir, is a matter of record, being the first judge before whom a case was tested, which resulted in favor of the South. And I go further than this; I hold as a just construction of the law, that not only has the slaveholder a right to reclaim his slave when and wherever found, but by its provision every free black in the country, North and South, are liable to enslavement by any white person. They are freemen by sufferance or slaves-at-large, whom any white person may claim at discretion. It was a just decision of the Supreme Court—though I was in advance of it by action—that persons of African descent have no rights that white men are bound to respect!"

"Judge Ballard, with this explanation, I am satisfied; indeed as a Southern man I would say, that you've conceded all that I could ask, and more than we expected. But this is a legal disquisition; what is your private opinion respecting the justice of the measures?"

"I think them right, sir, according to our system of government."

"But how will you get away from your representative system, Judge? In this your blacks are either voters, or reckoned among the inhabitants."

"Very well, sir, they stand in the same relation as your Negroes. In some of the states they are permitted to vote, but can't be voted for, and this leaves them without any political rights at all. Suffrage, sir, is one thing, franchisement another; the one a mere privilege—a thing permitted—the other a right inherent, that which is inviolable—cannot be interfered with. And my good sir, enumeration is a national measure, for which we are not sectionally responsible."

"Well, Judge, I'm compelled to admit that you are a very good Southerner; upon the whole, you are severe upon the Negroes; you seem to allow them no chance."

"I like Negroes well enough in their place!"

"How can you reconcile yourself to the state of things in Cuba, where the blacks enter largely into the social system?"

"I don't like it at all, and never could become reconciled to the state of things there. I consider that colony as it now stands, a moral pestilence, a blighting curse, and it is useless to endeavor to disguise the fact; Cuba must cease to be a Spanish colony, and become American territory. Those mongrel Creoles are incapable of self-government, and should be compelled to submit to the United States."

"Well, Judge, admit the latter part of that, as I rather guess we are all of the same way of thinking—how do you manage to get on with society when you are there?"

"I cannot for a moment tolerate it! One of the hateful customs of the place is that you must exchange civilities with whomsoever solicits it, consequently, the most stupid and ugly Negro you meet in the street may ask for a 'light' from your cigar."

"I know it, and I invariably comply with the request. How do you act in such cases?"

"I invariably comply, but as invariably throw away my cigar! If this were all, it would not be so bad, then the idea of meeting Negroes and mulattoes at the levees of the Captain General is intolerable! It will never do to permit this state of things so near our own shores."

"Why throw away the cigar, Judge? What objection could there be to it because a negro took a light from it?"

"Because they are certain to take hold of it with their black fingers!"

"Just as I've always heard, Judge Ballard. You Northerners are a great deal more fastidious about Negroes than we of the South, and you'll pardon me if I add, 'more nice than wise,' to use a homily. Did ever it occur to you that black fingers made that cigar, before it entered your white lips!—all tobacco preparations being worked by Negro hands in Cuba—and very frequently in closing up the wrapper, they draw it through their lips to give it tenacity."

"The deuce! Is that a fact, Major!"

"Does that surprise you, Judge? I'm sure the victuals you eat is cooked by black hands, the bread kneaded and made by black hands, and the sugar and molasses you use, all pass through black hands, or rather the hands of Negroes pass through them; at least you could not refrain from thinking so, had you seen them as I have frequently, with arms full length immersed in molasses."

"Well, Major, truly there are some things we are obliged to swallow, and I suppose these are among them."

"Though a Judge, Your Honor, you perceive that there are some things you have not learned."

"True, Major, true; and I like the Negro well enough in his place, but there is a disposition peculiar to the race, to shove themselves into the notice of the whites."

"Not peculiar to them, Judge, but common to mankind. The black man desires association with the white, because the latter is regarded his superior. In the South it is the poor white man with the wealthy, and in Europe the common with the gentlefolks. In the North you have not made these distinctions among the whites, which prevents you from noticing this trait among yourselves."

"Tell me, Major, as you seem so well to understand them, why a Negro swells so soon into importance?"

"Simply because he's just like you, Judge, and I! It is simply a manifestation of human nature in an humble position, the same as that developed in the breast of a conqueror. Our strictures are not just on this unfortunate race, as we condemn in them that which we approve in ourselves. Southerner as I am, I can joke with a slave just because he is a man; some of them indeed, fine warmhearted fellows, and intelligent, as was the Colonel's Henry."

"I can't swallow that, Major! Joking with a Negro is rather too large a dose for me!"

"Let me give you an idea of my feeling about these things: I have on my place two good-natured black fellows, full of pranks and jokes— Bob and Jef. Passing along one morning Jef was approaching me, when just as we met and I was about to give him the time of day, he made a sudden halt, placing himself in the attitude of a pugilist, grasping the muscle of his left arm, looking me full in the eyes exclaimed, 'Maus Army, my arm aches for you!' when stepping aside he gave the path for me to pass by."

"Did you not rebuke him for the impudence?"

"I laid my hand upon his shoulders as we passed, and gave him a laugh instead. At another time, passing along in company, Bob was righting up a section of fence, when Jef came along. 'How is yeh, Jef?' saluted Bob, without a response. Supposing he had not seen me, I hallooed out: 'How are you Jef!' but to this, he made no reply. A gentleman in company with me who enjoyed the joke, said: 'Why Jef, you appear to be above speaking to your old friends!' Throwing his head slightly down with a rocking motion in his walk, elongating his mouth after the manner of a sausage—which by the way needed no improvement in that direction—in a tone of importance still looking down he exclaimed, 'I totes a meat!' He had indeed, a fine gammon on his shoulder from which that evening, he doubtless intended a good supper with his wife, which made him feel important, just as Judge Ballard feels, when he receives the news that 'sugar is up,' and contemplates large profits from his crop of that season."

"I'll be plagued, Major, if your love of the ludicrous don't induce you to give the freest possible license to your Negroes! I wonder they respect you!"

"One thing, Judge, I have learned by my intercourse with men, that pleasantry is the life and soul of the social system; and good treatment begets more labor from the slave than bad. A smile from the master is better than cross looks, and one crack of a joke with him is worth a hundred cracks of the whip. Only confide in him, and let him be satisfied that you respect him as a man, he'll work himself to death to prove his worthiness."

"After all, Major, you still hold them as slaves, though you claim for them the common rights of other people!"

"Certainly! And I would just as readily hold a white as a black in slavery, were it the custom and policy of the country to do so. It is all a matter of self-interest with me; and though I am morally opposed to slavery, yet while the thing exists, I may as well profit by it, as others."

"Well, Major," concluded the Judge, "let us drop the subject, and I hope that the free interchange of opinion will prove no detriment to our future prospects and continued friendship."

"Not at all, sir, not at all!" concluded the Major with a smile.

Chapter 16

Solicitude and Amusement

Mrs. Franks sought the earliest opportunity for an interview with the Major concerning her favorite, Maggie. The children now missed her, little George continued fretful, and her own troubled soul was pressed with anxiety.

On conversing with the Major, to her great surprise she learned that the maid had been sold to a stranger, which intelligence he received from Mrs. Ballard herself, whom he met on the quay as he left Havana. The purchaser was a planter formerly of Louisiana, a bachelor by the name of Peter Labonier. This person resided twelve miles from Havana, the proprietor of a sugar estate.

The apprehension of Mrs. Franks, on learning these facts, were aroused to a point of fearful anxiety. These fears were mitigated by the probable chance, in her favor by a change of owners, as his first day's possession of her, turned him entirely against her. He would thus most probably part with her, which favored the desires of Mrs. Franks.

She urged upon the Major as a favor to herself, to procure the release of Maggie, by his purchase and enfranchisement with free papers of unconditional emancipation.

To this Major Armsted gave the fullest assurance, at the earliest possible opportunity. The company were to meet at no distant day, when he hoped to execute the orders.

"How did you leave cousin Arabella, Judge?" enquired Mrs. Franks, as he and the Colonel entered the parlor directly from the back porch, where they had been engaged for the last two hours in close conversation.

"Very well, Maria, when last heard from; a letter reaching me just before I left by the kindness of our mutual friend the Major. By the way, your girl and she did not get on so well, I be—!"

An admonitory look from Franks arrested the subject before the sentence was completed.

Every reference to the subject was carefully avoided, though the Colonel ventured to declare that henceforth towards his servants, instead of leniency, he intended severity. They were becoming every day more and more troublesome, and less reliable. He intended, in the language of his friend the Judge, to "lay upon them a heavy hand" in future.

"I know your sentiments on this point," he said in reply to an admonition from Armsted, "and I used to entertain the same views, but experience has taught me better."

"I shall not argue the point Colonel, but let you have your own way!" replied Armsted.

"Well, Judge, as you wish to become a Southerner; you must first 'see the sights,' as children say, and learn to get used to them. I wish you to ride out with me to Captain Grason's, and you'll see some rare sport; the most amusing thing I ever witnessed," suggested Franks.

"What is it?" enquired the Major.

"The effect is lost by previous knowledge of the thing," replied he. "This will suit you, Armsted, as you're fond of Negro jokes."

"Then, Colonel, let's be off," urged the Major.

"Off it is!" replied Franks, as he invited the gentlemen to take a seat in the carriage already at the door.

"Halloo, halloo, here you are, Colonel! Why Major Armsted, old fellow, 'pon my word!" saluted Grason, grasping Armsted by the hand as they entered the porch.

"Judge Ballard, sir," said Armsted.

"Just in time for dinner, gentlemen! Be seated," invited he, holding the Judge by the hand. "Welcome to Mississippi, Sir! What's up, gentlemen?"

"We've come out to witness some rare sport the Colonel has been telling us about," replied the Major.

"Blamed if I don't think the Colonel will have me advertised as a showman presently! I've got a queer animal here; I'll show him to you after dinner," rejoined Grason. "Gentlemen, help yourself to brandy and water."

Dinner over, the gentlemen walked into the pleasure grounds, in the rear of the mansion.

"Nelse, where is Rube? Call him!" said Grason to a slave lad, brother to the boy he sent for.

Shortly there came forward, a small black boy about eleven years of age, thin visage, projecting upper teeth, rather ghastly consumptive look, and emaciated condition. The child trembled with fear as he approached the group.

"Now gentlemen," said Grason, "I'm going to show you a sight!"

having in his hand a long whip, the cracking of which he commenced, as a ringmaster in the circus.

The child gave him a look never to be forgotten; a look beseeching mercy and compassion. But the decree was made, and though humanity quailed in dejected supplication before him, the command was imperative, with no living hand to stay the pending consequences. He must submit to his fate, and pass through the ordeal of training.

"Wat maus gwine do wid me now? I know wat maus gwine do," said this miserable child, "he gwine make me see sights!" when going down on his hands and feet, he commenced trotting around like an animal.

"Now gentlemen, look!" said Grason. "He'll whistle, sing songs, hymns, pray, swear like a trooper, laugh, and cry, all under the same state of feelings."

With a peculiar swing of the whip, bringing the lash down upon a certain spot on the exposed skin, the whole person being prepared for the purpose, the boy commenced to whistle almost like a thrush; another cut changed it to a song, another to a hymn, then a pitiful prayer, when he gave utterance to oaths which would make a Christian shudder, after which he laughed outright; then from the fullness of his soul he cried:

"O maussa, I's sick! Please stop little!" casting up gobs of hemorrhage.

Franks stood looking on with unmoved muscles. Armsted stood aside whittling a stick; but when Ballard saw, at every cut the flesh turn open in gashes streaming down with gore, till at last in agony he appealed for mercy, he involuntarily found his hand with a grasp on the whip, arresting its further application.

"Not quite a Southerner yet Judge, if you can't stand that!" said Franks on seeing him wiping away the tears.

"Gentlemen, help yourself to brandy and water. The little Negro don't stand it nigh so well as formerly. He used to be a trump!"

"Well, Colonel," said the Judge, "as I have to leave for Jackson this evening, I suggest that we return to the city."

The company now left Grason's, Franks for the enjoyment of home, Ballard and Armsted for Jackson, and the poor boy Reuben, from hemorrhage of the lungs, that evening left time for eternity.

Chapter 17

Henry at Large

On leaving the plantation carrying them hanging upon his arm, thrown across his shoulders, and in his hands Henry had a bridle, halter, blanket, girt, and horsewhip, the emblems of a faithful servant in discharge of his master's business.

By shrewdness and discretion—such was his management as he passed along—that he could tell the name of each place and proprietor long before he reached them. Being a scholar, he carefully kept a record of the plantations he had passed, that when accosted by a white, as an overseer or patrol, he invariably pretended to belong to a back estate, in search of his master's racehorse. If crossing a field, he was taking a near cut; but if met in a wood, the animal was in the forest, as being a great leaper no fence could debar him, though the forest was fenced and posted. The blanket, a substitute for a saddle, was in reality carried for a bed.

With speed unfaltering and spirits unflinching, his first great strive was to reach the Red River, to escape from his own state as quickly as possible. Proceeding on in the direction of the Red River country, he met with no obstruction except in one instance, when he left his assailant quietly upon the earth. A few days after an inquest was held upon the body of a deceased overseer—verdict of the Jury, "By hands unknown."

On approaching the river, after crossing a number of streams, as the Yazoo, Ouchita, and such, he was brought to sad reflections. A dread came over him, difficulties lay before him, dangers stood staring him in the face at every step he took. Here for the first time since his maturity of manhood responsibilities rose up in a shape of which he had no conception. A mighty undertaking, such as had never before been ventured upon, and the duty devolving upon him, was too much for a slave with no other aid than the aspirations of his soul panting for liberty. Reflecting upon the peaceful hours he once enjoyed as a professing Christian, and the distance which slavery had driven him from its peaceful portals, here in the wilderness, determining to renew his faith and dependence upon Divine aid, when falling upon his knees he opened his heart to God, as a tenement of the Holy Spirit.

"Arm of the Lord, awake! Renew my faith, confirm my hope, perfect me in love. Give strength, give courage, guide and protect my pathway, and direct me in my course!" Springing to his feet as if a weight had fallen from him, he stood up a new man.

The river is narrow, the water red as if colored by iron rust, the channel winding. Beyond this river lie his hopes, the broad plains of Louisiana with a hundred thousand bondsmen seeming anxiously to await him.

Standing upon a high bank of the stream, contemplating his mission, a feeling of humbleness and a sensibility of unworthiness impressed him, and that religious sentiment which once gave comfort to his soul now inspiring anew his breast, Henry raised in solemn tones amidst the lonely wilderness:

> *Could I but climb where Moses stood,*
> *And view the landscape o'er;*
> *Not Jordan's streams, nor death's cold flood,*
> *Could drive me from the shore!*

To the right of where he stood was a cove, formed by the washing of the stream at high water, which ran quite into the thicket, into which the sun shone through a space among the high trees.

While thus standing and contemplating his position, the water being too deep to wade, and on account of numerous sharks and alligators, too dangerous to swim, his attention was attracted by the sound of a steamer coming up the channel. Running into the cove to shield himself, a singular noise disturbed him, when to his terror he found himself amidst a squad of huge alligators, which sought the advantages of the sunshine.

His first impulse was to surrender himself to his fate and be devoured, as in the rear and either side the bank was perpendicular, escape being impossible except by the way he entered, to do which would have exposed him to the view of the boat, which could not have been avoided. Meantime the frightful animals were crawling over and among each other, at a fearful rate.

Seizing the fragment of a limb which lay in the cove, beating upon the ground and yelling like a madman, giving them all possible space, the beasts were frightened at such a rate, that they reached the water in less time than Henry reached the bank. Receding into the forest, he thus escaped the observation of the passing steamer, his escape serving to strengthen his fate in a renewed determination of spiritual dependence.

While gazing upon the stream in solemn reflection for Divine aid to direct him, logs came floating down, which suggested a proximity to the raft with which sections of that stream is filled, when going but a short distance up, he crossed in safety to the Louisiana side. His faith was now fully established, and thenceforth, Henry was full of hope and confident of success.

Reaching Alexandria with no obstruction, his first secret meeting was held in the hut of aunt Dilly. Here he found them all ready for an issue.

"An dis you, chile?" said the old woman, stooping with age, sitting on a low stool in the chimney corner. "Dis many day, I heahn on yeh!" though Henry had just entered on his mission. From Alexandria he passed rapidly on to Latuer's, making no immediate stops, preferring to organize at the more prominent places.

This is a mulatto planter, said to have come from the isle of Guadaloupe. Riding down the road upon a pony at a quick gallop was a mulatto youth, a son of the planter, an old black man on foot keeping close to the horse's heels.

"Whose boy are you?" enquired the young mulatto, who had just dismounted, the old servant holding his pony.

"I'm in search of master's race horse."

"What is your name?" further enquired the young mulatto.

"Gilbert, sir."

"What do you want?"

"I am hungry, sir."

"Dolly," said he to an old black woman at the woodpile, "show this man into the Negro quarter, and give him something to eat; give him a cup of milk. Do you like milk, my man?"

"Yes, sir, I have no choice when hungry; anything will do."

"Da is none heah but claubah, maus Eugene," replied the old cook.

"Give him that," said the young master. "You people like that kind of stuff I believe; our Negroes like it."

"Yes, sir," replied Henry when the lad left.

"God knows 'e needn' talk 'bout wat we po' black folks eat, case da don' ghin us nothin' else but dat an' caun bread," muttered the old woman.

"Don't they treat you well, aunty?" enquired Henry.

"God on'y knows, my chile, wat we suffeh."

"Who was that old man who ran behind your master's horse?"

"Dat Nathan, my husban'."

"Do they treat him well, aunty?"

"No, chile, wus an' any dog, da beat 'im foh little an nothin'."

"Is uncle Nathan religious?"

"Yes, chile, ole man an' I's been sahvin' God dis many day, fo yeh baun! Wen any one on 'em in de house git sick, den da sen foh 'uncle Nathan' come pray foh dem; 'uncle Nathan' mighty good den!"

"Do you know that the Latuers are colored people?"

"Yes, chile; God bless yeh soul yes! Case huh mammy ony dead two-three yehs, an' she black as me."

"How did they treat her?"

"Not berry well; she nus da childen; an eat in a house arter all done."

"What did Latuer's children call her?"

"Da call huh 'mammy' same like wite folks childen call de nus."

"Can you tell me, aunty, why they treat you people so badly, knowing themselves to be colored, and some of the slaves related to them?"

"God bless yeh, hunny, de wite folks, dese plantehs make 'em so; da run heah, an' tell 'em da mus'n treat deh niggers well, case da spile 'em."

"Do the white planters frequently visit here?"

"Yes, hunny, yes, da heah some on 'em all de time eatin' an' drinkin' long wid de old man; da on'y tryin' git wat little 'e got, dat all! Da 'tend to be great frien' de ole man; but laws a massy, hunny, I doh mine dese wite folks no how!"

"Does your master ever go to their houses and eat with them?"

"Yes, chile, some time 'e go, but den half on 'em got nothin' fit to eat; da hab fat poke an' bean, caun cake an' sich like, dat all da got, some on 'em."

"Does Mr. Latuer give them better at his table?"

"Laws, hunny, yes; yes'n deed, chile! 'E got mutton—some time whole sheep mos'—fowl, pig, an' ebery tum ting a nuddeh, 'e got so much ting dah, I haudly know wat cook fus."

"Do the white planters associate with the family of Latuer?"

"One on 'em, ten 'e coatin de dahta; I don't recon 'e gwine hab heh. Da cah fool long wid 'Toyeh's gals dat way."

"Whose girls, Metoyers?"

"Yes, chile."

"Do you mean the wealthy planters of that name?"

"Dat same, chile.'

"Well, I want to understand you; you don't mean to say that they are colored people?"

"Yes, hunny, yes; da good culed folks anybody. Some five-six boys' an five-six gals on 'em; da all rich."

"How do they treat their slaves?"

"Da boys all mighty haud maustas, de gals all mighty good; sahvants all like 'em."

"You seem to understand these people very well, aunty. Now please tell me what kind of masters there are generally in the Red River country."

"Haud 'nough, chile, haud 'nough, God on'y knows!"

"Do the colored masters treat theirs generally worse than the whites?"

"No, hunny, 'bout da same."

"That's just what I want to know. What are the usual allowances for slaves?"

"Da 'low de fiel' han' two suit a yeah; foh umin one long linen coat, make suit; an' foh man, pantaloon an' jacket."

"How about eating?"

"Half-peck meal ah day foh family uh fo!"

"WHAT ABOUT WEEKLY PRIVILEGES? Do you have Saturday to yourselves?"

"Laud, honny, no! No, chile, no! Da do'n 'low us no time, 'tall. Da 'low us ebery uddeh Sunday wash ouh close; dat all de time we git."

"Then you don't get to sell anything for yourselves?"

"No, hunny, no. Da don' 'low pig, chicken, tucky, goose, bean, pea, tateh, nothin' else."

"Well, aunty. I'm glad to meet you, and as evening's drawing nigh, I must see your husband a little, then go."

"God bless yeh, chile, whah ebeh yeh go! Yeh ain' arteh no racehos, dat yeh ain't."

"You got something to eat, my man, did you?" enquired the lad Eugene, at the conclusion of his interview with uncle Nathan.

"I did, sir, and feasted well!" replied Henry in conclusion. "Good bye!" and he left for the next plantation suited to his objects.

"God bless de baby!" said old aunt Dolly as uncle Nathan entered the hut, referring to Henry.

"Ah, chile!" replied the old man with tears in his eyes; "my yeahs has heahn dis day!"

Chapter 18

Fleeting Shadows

In high spirits Henry left the plantation of Latuer, after sowing seeds from which in due season, he anticipated an abundant harvest. He found the old man Nathan all that could be desired, and equal to the task of propagating the scheme. His soul swelled with exultation on receiving the tidings, declaring that though nearly eighty years of age, he never felt before an implied meaning, in the promise of the Lord.

"Now Laud!" with uplifted hand exclaimed he at the conclusion of the interview. "My eyes has seen, and meh yeahs heahn, an' now Laud! I's willin' to stan' still an' see dy salvation!"

On went Henry to Metoyers, visiting the places of four brothers, having taken those of the white planters intervening, all without detection or suspicion of being a stranger.

Stopping among the people of Colonel Hopkins at Grantico summit, here as at Latuer's and all intermediate places, he found the people patiently looking for a promised redemption. Here a pet female slave, Silva, espied him and gave the alarm that a strange black was lurking among the Negro quarters, which compelled him to retirement sooner than intended.

Among the people of Dickson at Pine Bluff, he found the best of spirits. There was Newman, a young slave man born without arms, who was ready any moment for a strike.

"How could you fight?" said Henry. "You have no arms!"

"I am compelled to pick with my toes, a hundred pound of cotton a day, and I can sit on a stool and touch off a cannon!" said this promising young man whose heart panted with an unsuppressed throb for liberty.

Heeley's, Harrison's, and Hickman's slaves were fearfully and pitiably dejected. Much effort was required to effect a seclusion, and more to stimulate them to action. The continual dread "that maus wont let us!" seemed as immovably fixed as the words were constantly repeated; and it was not until an occasion for another subject of inquest, in the person of a pest of an old black slave man, that an organization was effected.

Approaching Crane's on Little River, the slaves were returning from the field to the gin. Many—being females, some of whom were very handsome—had just emptied their baskets. So little clothing had they, and so loosely hung the tattered fragments about them, that they covered themselves behind the large empty baskets tilted over on the side, to shield their person from exposure.

The overseer engaged in another direction, the master absent, and the family at the great house, a good opportunity presented for an inspection of affairs.

"How do you do, young woman?" saluted Henry.

"How de do, sir!" replied a sprightly, comely young mulatto girl, who stood behind her basket with not three yards of cloth in the tattered relic of the only garment she had on.

"Who owns this place?"

"Mr. Crane, sir," she politely replied with a smile.

"How many slaves has he?"

"I don'o, some say five 'a six hunded."

"Do they all work on this place?"

"No, sir, he got two-three places."

"How many on this place?"

"Oveh a hundred an' fifty."

"What allowances have you?"

"None, sir."

"What! no Saturday to yourselves?"

"No, sir."

"They allow you Sundays, I suppose."

"No, sir, we work all day ev'ry Sunday."

"How late do you work?"

"Till we can' see to pick no mo' cotton; but w'en its moon light we pick till ten o'clock at night."

"What time do you get to wash your clothes?"

"None, sir; da on'y 'low us one suit ev'ry New Yehs day, an' us gals take it off every Satady night aftah de men all gone to bed and wash it fah Sunday."

"Why do you want clean clothes on Sunday, if you have to work on that day?"

"It's de Laud's day, an' we wa to be clean, and we feel betteh."

"How do the men do for clean clothes?"

"We wash de men's clothes afteh da go to bed."

"And you say you are only allowed one suit a year? Now, young woman, I don't know your name but—"

"Nancy, sir."

"Well, Nancy, speak plainly, and dont be backward; what does your one suit consist of?"

"A frock, sir, made out er coarse tow linen."

"Only one piece, and no underclothes at all?"

"Dat's all, sir!" replied she modestly looking down and drawing the basket, which sufficiently screened her, still closer to her person.

"Is that which you have on a sample of the goods your clothes are made of?"

"Yes, sir, dis is da kine."

"I would like to see some other of your girls."

"Stop, sir, I go call Susan!" when, gathering up and drawing around and before her a surplus of the back section, the only remaining sound remnant of the narrow tattered garment that she wore, off she ran behind the gin, where lay in the sun, a number of girls to rest themselves during their hour of "spell."

"Susan!" she exclaimed rather loudly. "I do'n want you gals!" she pleasantly admonished, as the whole twelve or fifteen rose from their resting place, and came hurriedly around the building, Nancy and Susan in the lead. They instinctively as did Nancy, drew their garments around and about them, on coming in sight of the stranger. Standing on the outside of the fence, Henry politely bowed as they approached.

"Dis is Susan, sir!" said Nancy, introducing her friend with bland simplicity.

"How de do, sir!" saluted she, a modest and intelligent, very pretty young black girl, of good address.

"Well, Susan!" replied Henry. "I don't want anything but to see you girls; but I will ask you this question: how many suits of clothes do they give you a year?"

"One, sir."

"How many pieces make a suit?"

"Jus' one frock," and they simultaneously commenced drawing still closer before, the remnant of coarse garment, which hung in tatters about them.

"Don't you have shoes and stockings in winter?"

"We no call foh shoes, case 'taint cole much; on'y some time little fros'."

"How late in the evening do you work?"

"Da fiel' han's dah," pointing to those returning to the field, "da work till bedtime, but we gals heah, we work in de gin, and spell each other ev'ey twelve ouahs."

"You're at leisure now; who fills your places?"

"Nutha set a' han's go to work, fo' you come."

"How much cotton do they pick for a task?"

"Each one mus' pick big basket full, an' fetch it in f'om da fiel' to de gin, else da git thirty lashes."

"How much must the women pick as a task?"

"De same as de men."

"That can't be possible!" said Henry, looking over the fence down upon their baskets. "How much do they hold?"

"I dis membeh sir, but good 'eal."

"I see on each basket marked 225 pounds; is that the quantity they hold?"

"Yes, sir, dat's it."

"All mus' be in gin certain ouah else da git whipped; sometime de men help 'em."

"How can they do this when they have their own to carry?"

"Da put derse on de head, an' ketch holt one side de women basket. Sometimes they leave part in de fiel', an' go back afteh it."

"Do you get plenty to eat?"

"No, sir, da feeds us po'ly; sometime, we do'n have mo'n half nough!"

"Did you girls ever work in the field?"

"O yes, sir! all uv us, on'y we wan't strong nough to fetch in ouh cotton, den da put us in de gin."

"Where would you rather; in the gin or in the field?"

"If 'twant foh carryin' cotton, we'a rather work in de fiel'."

"Why so, girls?"

"Case den da would'n be so many ole wite plantehs come an' look at us, like we was show!"

"Who sees that the tasks are all done in the field?"

"Da Driveh."

"Is he a white man?"

"No sir, black."

"Is he a free man?"

"No, sir, slave."

"Have you no white overseer?"

"Yes, sir, Mr. Dorman."

"Where is Dorman when you are at work."

"He out at de fiel too."

"What is he doing there?"

"He watch Jesse, da drivah."

"Is Jesse a pretty good fellow?"

"No, sir, he treat black folks like dog, he all de time beat 'em, when da no call to do it."

"How did he treat you girls when you worked in the field?"

"He beat us if we jist git little behind de rest in pickin'! Da wite folks make 'im bad."

"Point him out to me and after tonight, he'll never whip another."

"Now, girls, I see that you are smart intelligent young women, and I want you to tell me why it is, that your master keeps you all here at work in the gin, when he could get high prices for you, and supply your places with common cheap hands at half the money?"

"Case we gals won' go! Da been mo'n a dozen plantehs heah lookin' at us, an' want to buy us foh house keepehs, an' we wont go; we die fus!" said Susan with a shudder.

"Yes," repeated Nancy, with equal emotion, "we die fus!"

"How can you prevent it, girls; won't your master sell you against your will?"

"Yes, sir, he would, but da plantehs da don't want us widout we willin' to go."

"I see! Well girls, I believe I'm done with you; but before leaving let me ask you, is there among your men, a real clever good trusty man? I don't care either old or young, though I prefer an old or middle-aged man."

"O yes, sir," replied Nancy, "da is some mong 'em."

"Give me the name of one," said Henry, at which request Nancy and Susan looked hesitatingly at each other.

"Don't be backward," admonished he, "as I shan't make a bad use of it." But still they hesitated, when after another admonition Nancy said, "Dare's uncle Joe—"

"No, uncle Moses, uncle Moses!" in a suppressed tone interrupted the other girls.

"Who is uncle Moses?" enquired Henry.

"He' my fatha," replied Susan, "an—"

"My uncle!" interrupted Nancy.

"Then you two are cousins?"

"Yes, sir, huh fatha an my motha is brotha an sisteh," replied Nancy.

"Is he a religious man, girls?"

"Yes, sir, he used to preach but'e do'n preach now," explained Susan.

"Why?"

"Case da 'ligions people wo'n heah im now."

"Who, colored people?"

"Yes, sir."

"When did they stop hearing him preach?"

"Good while ago."

"Where at?"

"Down in da bush meetin', at da Baptism."

"He's a Baptist then—what did he do?"

Again became Susan and Nancy more perplexed than before, the other girls in this instance failing to come to their relief.

"What did he do girls? Let me know it quick, as I must be off!"

"Da say—da say—I do'n want tell you!" replied Susan hesitating, with much feeling.

"What is it girls, can't some of you tell me?" earnestly enquired Henry.

"Da say befo' 'e come heah way down in Fagina, he kill a man, ole po' wite ovehseeah!"

"Is that it, girls?" enquired he.

"Yes, sir!" they simultaneously replied.

"Then he's the very man I want to see!" said Henry. "Now don't forget what I say to you; tell him that a man will meet him tonight below here on the river side, just where the carcass of an ox lies in the verge of the thicket. Tell him to listen and when I'm ready, I'll give the signal of a runaway—the screech of the panther—when he must immediately obey the summons. One word more, and I'll leave you. Every one of you as you have so praiseworthily concluded, die before surrendering to such base purposes as that for which this man who holds you wishes to dispose of you. Girls, you will see me no more. Fare—"

"Yo' name sir, yo' name!" they all exclaimed.

"My name is—Farewell, girls, farewell!"—when Henry darted in the thickest of the forest, leaving the squad of young maiden slaves in a state of bewildering inquiry concerning the singular black man.

The next day Jesse the driver was missed, and never after heard of. On inquiry being made of the old man Moses concerning the stranger, all that could be elicited was, "Stan' still child'en, and see da salvation uv da Laud!"

Chapter 19

Come What Will

Leaving the plantation of Crane with high hopes and great confidence in the integrity of uncle Moses and the maiden gang of cotton girls, Henry turned his course in a retrograde direction so as again to take the stream of Red River, Little River, where he then was, being but a branch of that water.

Just below its confluence with the larger stream, at the moment when he reached the junction, a steam cotton trader hove in view. There was no alternative but to stand like a freeman, or suddenly escape into the forest, thus creating suspicions and fears, as but a few days previous a French planter of the neighborhood lost a desperate slave, who became a terror to the country around. The master was compelled to go continually armed, as also other white neighbors, and all were afraid after nightfall to pass out the threshold of their own doors. Permission was given to every white man to shoot him if ever seen within rifle shot, which facts having learned the evening before, Henry was armed with this precaution.

His dress being that of a racegroom—small leather cap with long front piece, neat fitting roundabout, high boots drawn over the pantaloon legs, with blanket, girth, halter, whip and bridle—Henry stood upon the shore awaiting the vessel.

"Well boy!" hailed the captain as the line was thrown out, which he caught, making fast at the root of a tree. "Do you wish to come aboard?"

"Good man!" approvingly cried the mate, at the expert manner which he caught the line and tied the sailor knot.

"Have you ever steamboated, my man?" continued the captain.

"Yes, sir," replied Henry.

"Where?"

"On the Upper and Lower Mississippi, sir."

"Whom do you know as masters of steamers on the Upper Mississippi?"

"Captains Thogmorton, Price, Swan, and—"

"Stop, stop! That'll do," interrupted the captain, "you know the master of every steamer in the trade, I believe. Now who in the Lower trade?"

MARTIN R. DELANY

"Captains Scott, Hart, and—"

"What's Captain Hart's Christian name?" interrupted the captain.

"Jesse, sir."

"That'll do, by George you know everybody! Do you want to ship?"

"No, sir."

"What are you doing here?"

"I'm hunting master's stray racehorse."

"Your master's race horse! Are you a slave boy?"

"Yes, sir."

"How did you come to be on the Mississippi River?"

"I hired my time, sir."

"Yes, yes, boy, I see!"

"Who is your master?"

"Colonel Sheldon; I used to belong to Major Gilmore."

"Are you the boy Nepp, the great horse trainer the Major used to own?"

"No, sir, I'm his son."

"Are you as good at training horses as the old chap?"

"They call me better, sir."

"Then you're worth your weight in gold. Will your master sell you?"

"I don't know, sir."

"How did your horse come to get away?"

"He was bought from the Major by Colonel Sheldon to run at the great Green Wood Races, Texas, and while training he managed to get away, leaping the fences, and taking to the forest."

"Then you're Major Tom's race rider Gilbert! You're a valuable boy; I wonder the Major parted with you."

The bell having rung for dinner, the captain left, Henry going to the deck.

Among those on deck was a bright mulatto young man, who immediately recognized Henry as having seen him on the Upper Mississippi, he being a free man. On going up to him, Henry observed that he was laden with heavy manacles.

"Have I not seen you somewhere before?" enquired he.

"Yes; my name is Lewis Grimes, you saw me on the Upper Mississippi," replied the young man. "Your name is Henry Holland!"

"What have you been doing?" enquired Henry, on seeing the handcuffs.

"Nothing at all!" replied he with eyes flashing resentment and suffused with tears.

"What does this mean?" continued he, pointing at the handcuffs.

"I am stolen and now being taken to Texas, where I am to be enslaved for life!" replied Lewis sobbing aloud.

"Who did this vile deed?" continued Henry in a low tone of voice, pressing his lips to suppress his feelings.

"One Dr. Johns of Texas, now a passenger on this boat!"

"Was that the person who placed a glass to your lips which you refused, just as I came aboard?"

"Yes, that's the man."

"Why don't you leave him instantly?" said Henry, his breast heaving with emotion.

"Because he always handcuffs me before the boat lands, keeping me so during the time she lies ashore."

"Why don't you jump overboard when the boat is under way?"

"Because he guards me with a heavy loaded rifle, and I can't get a chance."

"He 'guards' you! 'You can't get a chance!' Are there no nights, and does he never sleep?"

"Yes, but he makes me sleep in the stateroom with him, keeping his rifle at his bedside."

"Are you never awake when he's asleep?"

"Often, but I'm afraid to stir lest he wakens."

"Well don't you submit, die first if thereby you must take another into eternity with you! Were it my case and he ever went to sleep where I was, he'd never waken in this world!"

"I never thought of that before, I shall take your advice the first opportunity. Good-bye sir!" hastily said the young man, as the bell tapped a signal to start, and Henry stepped on shore.

"Let go that line!" sternly commanded the captain, Henry obeying orders on the shore, when the boat glided steadily up the stream, seemingly in unison with the lively though rude and sorrowful song of the black firemen—

> *I'm a-goin' to Texas—O! O-O-O!*
> *I'm a-goin' to Texas—O! O-O-O!*

Having in consequence of the scarcity of spring houses and larders along his way in so level and thinly settled country, Henry took in his pouch from the cook of the boat an ample supply of provisions for the suceeding four or five days. Thus provided for, standing upon the bank for a few minutes, with steady gaze listening to the sad song of his oppressed brethren as they left the spot, and reflecting still more on the miserable fate of the young mulatto freeman Lewis Grimes held by the slave-holder Dr. Johns of Texas, he, with renewed energy, determined that nothing short of an interference by Divine Providence should stop his plans and progress. In soliloquy said Henry, "Yes!

> *If every foe stood martialed in the van,*
> *I'd fight them single combat, man to man!"*

and again he started with a manly will, as fixed and determined in his purpose as though no obstructions lay in his pathway.

From plantation to plantation did he go, sowing the seeds of future devastation and ruin to the master and redemption to the slave, an antecedent more terrible in its anticipation than the warning voice of the destroying Angel in commanding the slaughter of the firstborn of Egypt. Himself careworn, distressed and hungry, who just being supplied with nourishment for the system, Henry went forth a welcome messenger, casting his bread upon the turbid waters of oppression, in hopes of finding it after many days.

Holding but one seclusion on each plantation, his progress was consequently very rapid, in whatever direction he went.

With a bold stride from Louisiana, he went into Texas. Here he soon met with the man of his wishes. This presented in the person of Sampson, on the cotton place of proprietor Richardson. The master here, though represented wealthy, with an accomplished and handsome young daughter, was a silly, stupid old dolt, an inordinate blabber and wine bibber. The number of his slaves was said to be great and he the owner of three plantations, one in Alabama, and the others in Texas.

Sampson was a black, tall, stoutly built, and manly, possessing much general intelligence, and a good-looking person. His wife a neat, intelligent, handsome little woman, the complexion of himself, was the mother of a most interesting family of five pretty children, three boys and two girls. This family entered at once into the soul of his mission, seeming to have anticipated it.

With an amply supply of means, buried in a convenient well-marked spot, he only awaited a favorable opportunity to effect his escape from slavery. With what anxiety did that wife gaze smilingly in his face, and a boy and girl cling tightly each to a knee, as this husband and father in whispers recounted his plans and determination of carrying them out. The scheme of Henry was at once committed to his confidence, and he requested to impart them wherever he went.

Richardson was a sportsman and Sampson his body servant, they traveled through every part of the country, thus affording the greatest opportunity for propagating the measures of the secret organization. From Portland in Maine to Galveston in Texas, Sampson was as familiar as a civil engineer.

"Sampson, Sampson, stand by me! Stand by me, my man; stand at your master's back!" was the language of this sottish old imbecile he kept continually reveling at a gambling table, and who from excessive fatigue would sometimes squat or sit down upon the floor behind him. "Sampson, Sampson! are you there? Stand by your master, Sampson!" again would he exclaim, so soon as the tall commanding form of his black protector was missed from his sight.

Sampson and his wife were both pious people, believing much in the Providence of God, he, as he said, having recently had it "shown to" him—meaning a presentiment—that a messenger would come to him and reveal the plan of deliverance.

"I am glad to see that you have money," said Henry, "you are thereby well qualified for your mission. With money you may effect your escape almost at any time. Your most difficult point is an elevated obstruction, a mighty hill, a mountain; but through that hill there is a gap, and money is your passport through that White Gap to freedom. Mark that! It is the great range of White mountains and White river which are before you, and the White Gap that you must pass through to reach the haven of safety. Money alone will carry you through the White mountains or across the White river to liberty."

"Brother, my eyes is open, and my way clear!" responded Sampson to this advice.

"Then," said Henry, "you are ready to 'rise and shine' for—"

"My light has come!—" interrupted Sampson. "But—"

"The glory of God is not yet shed abroad!" concluded Henry, who fell upon Sampson's neck with tears of joy in meeting unexpectedly one of his race so intelligent in that region of country.

Sampson and wife Dursie, taking Henry by the hand wept aloud, looking upon him as the messenger of deliverance foreshown to them.

Kneeling down a fervent prayer was offered by Sampson for Henry's protection by the way, and final success in his "mighty plans," with many Amens and "God grants," by Dursie.

Partaking of a sumptuous fare on 'ash cake and sweet milk—a dainty diet with many slaves—and bidding with a trembling voice and tearful eye a final "Farewell!" in six hours he had left the state of Texas to the consequences of a deep-laid scheme for a terrible insurrection.

Chapter 20

ADVENT AMONG THE INDIANS

From Texas Henry went into the Indian Nation near Fort Towson, Arkansas.

"Make yourself at home, sir," invited Mr. Culver, the intelligent old Chief of the United Nation, "and Josephus will attend to you," referring to his nephew Josephus Braser, an educated young chief and counselor among his people.

"You are slaveholders, I see, Mr. Culver!" said Henry.

"We are, sir, but not like the white men," he replied.

"How many do you hold?"

"About two hundred on my two plantations."

"I can't well understand how a man like you can reconcile your principles with the holding of slaves and—"

"We have had enough of that!" exclaimed Dr. Donald, with a tone of threatening authority.

"Hold your breath, sir, else I'll stop it!" in a rage replied the young chief.

"Sir," responded the Doctor, "I was not speaking to you, but only speaking to that Negro!" "You're a fool!" roared Braser, springing to his feet.

"Come, come, gentlemen!" admonished the old Chief. "I think you are both going mad! I hope you'll behave something better."

"Well, uncle, I can't endure him! he assumes so much authority!" replied he. "He'll make the Indians slaves just now, then Negroes will have no friends."

Donald was a white man, married among the Indians a sister of the old Chief and aunt to the young, for the sake of her wealth and a home. A physician without talents, he was unable to make a business and unwilling to work.

"Mr. Bras—"

"I want nothing more of you," interrupted Braser, "and don't—"

"Josephus, Josephus!" interrupted the old chief. "You will surely let the Doctor speak!"

Donald stood pale and trembling before the young Choctaw born

MARTIN R. DELANY

to command, when receiving no favor he left the company muttering "nigger!"

"Now you see," said Mr. Culver as the Doctor left the room, "the difference between a white man and Indian holding slaves. Indian work side by side with black man, eat with him, drink with him, rest with him and both lay down in shade together; white man even won't let you talk! In our Nation Indian and black all marry together. Indian like black man very much, ony he don't fight 'nough. Black man in Florida fight much, and Indian like 'im heap!"

"You make, sir, a slight mistake about my people. They would fight if in their own country they were united as the Indians here, and not scattered thousands of miles apart as they are. You should also remember that the Africans have never permitted a subjugation of their country by foreigners as the Indians have theirs, and Africa today is still peopled by Africans, whilst America, the home of the Indian—who is fast passing away—is now possessed and ruled by foreigners."

"True, true!" said the old Chief, looking down reflectingly. "Too true! I had not thought that way before. Do you think the white man couldn't take Africa if he wanted?"

"He might by a combination, and I still am doubtful whether then he could if the Africans were determined as formerly to keep him out. You will also remember, that the whites came in small numbers to America, and then drove the Indians from their own soil, whilst the blacks got in Africa as slaves, are taken by their own native conquerors, and sold to white men as prisoners of war."

"That is true, sir, true!" sighed the old Chief. "The Indian, like game before the bow, is passing away before the gun of the white man!"

"What I now most wish to learn is, whether in case that the blacks should rise, they may have hope or fear from the Indian?" asked Henry.

"I'm an old mouthpiece, been puffing out smoke and talk many seasons for the entertainment of the young and benefit of all who come among us. The squaws of the great men among the Indians in Florida were black women, and the squaws of the black men were Indian women. You see the vine that winds around and holds us together. Don't cut it, but let it grow till bimeby, it git so stout and strong, with many, very many little branches attached, that you can't separate them. I now reach to you the pipe of peace and hold out the olive-branch of hope! Go on young man, go on. If you want white man to love you, you must fight im!" concluded the intelligent old Choctaw.

"Then, sir, I shall rest contented, and impart to you the object of my mission," replied Henry.

"Ah hah!" exclaimed the old chief after an hour's seclusion with him. "Ah hah! Indian have something like that long-go. I wonder your people ain't got it before! That what make Indian strong; that what make Indian and black man in Florida hold together. Go on young man, go on! may the Great Spirit make you brave!" exhorted Mr. Culver, when the parties retired for the evening, Henry rooming with the young warrior Braser.

By the aid of the young Chief and kindness of his uncle the venerable old brave, Henry was conducted quite through the nation on a pony placed at his service, affording to him an ample opportunity of examining into the condition of things. He left the settlement with the regrets of the people, being the only instance in which his seclusions were held with the master instead of the slave.

Chapter 21

WHAT NOT

Leaving the United Nation of Chickasaw and Choctaw Indians, Henry continued his travel in this the roughest, apparently, of all the states. Armed with bowie knives and revolvers openly carried belted around the person, he who displays the greatest number of deadly weapons seems to be considered the greatest man. The most fearful incivility and absence of refinement was apparent throughout this region. Neither the robes of state nor gown of authority is sufficient to check the vengeance of awakened wrath in Arkansas. Law is but a fable, its ministration a farce, and the pillars of justice but as stubble before the approach of these legal invaders.

Hurriedly passing on in the darkness of the night, Henry suddenly came upon a procession in the wilderness, slowly and silently marching on, the cortege consisting principally of horsemen, there being but one vehicle, advanced by four men on horseback. Their conversation seemed at intervals of low, muttering, awestricken voices. The vehicle was closely covered, and of a sad, heavy sound by the rattling of the wheels upon the unfinished path of the great Arkansas road. Here he sat in silence listening, waiting for the passage of the solemn procession, but a short distance from whence in the thicket stood the hut of the slave to whom he was sent.

"Ole umin! done yeh heah some 'un trampin' round de house? Hush! evedroppehs 'bout!" admonished Uncle Jerry.

"Who dat?" enquired Aunt Rachel, as Henry softly rapped at the back window.

"A friend!" was the reply.

"What saut frien' dat go sneak roun' people back windah stid comin' to de doh!"

"Hush, ole umin, yeh too fas'! how yeh know who 'tis? Frien', come roun' to de doh," said the old man.

Passing quickly around, the door was opened, a blazing hot fire shining full in his face, the old man holding in his hand a heavy iron poker in the attitude of defence.

"Is dis you, my frien'?" enquired Uncle Jerry, to whom Henry was an entire stranger.

"Yes, uncle, this is me," replied he.

"God bless yeh, honey! come in; we didn know 'twos you, chile! God bless de baby!" added Aunt Rachel. "Ole man, heah yeh comin' an' we been lookin' all day long. Dis evenin' I git some suppeh, an' I don'o if yeh come uh no."

"How did you know I was coming, aunty?"

"O! honey, da tell us," replied she.

"Who told you?"

"De folks up dah."

"Up where?"

"Up dah, 'mong de Injins, chile."

"Indians told you?"

"No, honey; some de black folks, da all'as gwine back and for'ard, and da lahn heap from dem up dah; an' da make 'ase an' tell us."

"Can you get word from each other so far apart, that easy?"

"Yes 'ndeed, honey! some on 'em all de time gwine; wite folks know nothin' 'bout it. Some time some on 'em gone two-three day, an' ain miss; white folks tink da in the woods choppin'."

"Why, that's the very thing! you're ahead of all the other states. You folks in Arkansas must be pretty well organized already."

"Wat dat yeh mean, chile, dat 'organ' so?"

"I mean by that, aunty, a good general secret understanding among yourselves."

"Ah, chile! dat da is. Da comin' all de time, ole man hardly time to eat mou'full wen 'e come in de hut night."

"Tell me, aunty, why people like you and uncle here, who seem to be at the head of these secrets, are not more cautious with me, a stranger?"

"Ole umin, I lisenin at yeh!" said Uncle Jerry, after enough had been told to betray them; but the old people well understood each other, Aunt Rachel by mutual consent being the mouthpiece.

"How we knows you!" rejoined the old woman. "Wy, chile, yeh got mahk dat so soon as we put eye on yeh, we knows yeh. Huccum yeh tink we gwine tell yeh so much wen we don'o who yeh is? Sho, chile, we ain't dat big fool!"

"Then you know my errand among you, aunty?"

"Yes, meh son, dat we does, an' we long been waitin' foh some sich like you to come 'mong us. We thang God dis night in ouh soul! We long been lookin' foh ye, chile!" replied Uncle Jerry.

"You are closely watched in this state, I should think, uncle."

"Yes, chile, de patrolas da all de time out an' gwine in de quahtehs an' huntin' up black folks wid der 'nigga-dogs' as da call 'em."

"I suppose you people scarcely ever get a chance to go anywhere, then?"

"God bless yeh, honey, da blacks do'n mine dem noh der 'niggadogs' nutha. Patrolas feahd uh de black folks, an' da black folks charm de dogs, so da cahn heht 'em," said Aunt Rachel.

"I see you understand yourselves! Now, what is my best way to get along through the state?"

"Keep in de thicket, chile, as da patrolas feahd to go in de woods, da feahd runaway ketch 'em! Keep in da woods, chile, an' da ain' goin' dah bit! Da talk big, and sen' der dog, but da ain' goin' honey!" continued the old woman.

"Ah spose, meh son, yeh know how to chaum dogs?" enquired Uncle Jerry.

"I understand the mixed bull, but not the full-bred Cuba dog," replied Henry.

"Well, chile, da keep boph kine heah, de bull dog an' bloodhoun' an' fo' yeh go, I lahn yeh how to fix 'em all! Da come sneakin' up to yeh! da cahn bite yeh!"

"Thank you, Uncle Jerry! I'll try and do as much for you in some way."

"Yeh no call foh dat, meh son; it ain' nothin' mo' nah onh—"

"Hush! ole man; ain' dat dem?" admonished Aunt Rachel, in a whisper, as she went to the door, thrusting out her head in the dark.

"Who? Patrols?" with anxiety enquired Henry.

"No, chile, de man da kill down yondah; all day long da been lookin' foh 'em to come."

"A procession passed just before I came to your door, which I took for a funeral."

"Yes, chile, dat's it, da kill im down dah.'

On enquiry, it appeared that in the senate a misunderstanding on the rules of order and parliamentary usage occurred, when the Speaker, conceiving himself insulted by the senator who had the floor, deliberately arose from his chair, when approaching the senator, drove a bowie knife through his body from the chest, which laid him a corpse upon the senate floor.

"There he is! There he is!" stormed the assassin, pointing with defiance at the lifeless body, his hand still reeking with blood. "I did it!" slapping his hand upon his own breast in triumph of his victory.

They had just returned with the body of the assassinated statesman to the wretched home of his distracted family, some ten miles beyond the hut of Uncle Jerry.

"Is this the way they treat each other, aunty?"

"Yes, chile, wus den dat! da kill one-notha in cole blood, sometime at de table eatin'. Da all'as choppin' up some on 'em."

"Then you black people must have a poor chance among them, if this is the way they do each other!"

"Mighty po', honey; mighty po' indeed!" replied Uncle Jerry.

"Well, uncle, it's now time I was doing something; I've been here some time resting. Aunty, see to your windows and door; are there any cracks in the walls!"

"No, honey, da dob good!" whispered the old woman as a wellpatched, covering quilt to shield the door was hung, covering nearly one side of the hut, and a thickly-patched linsey gown fully shielded the only window of four eight-by-ten lights.

These precautions taken, they drew together in a corner between the head of the bed and well-daubed wall to hold their seclusion.

"Laud!" exclaimed Uncle Jerry, after the secrets were fully imparted to them. "Make beah dine all-conquering ahm! strike off de chains dat dy people may go free! Come, Laud, a little nigh, eh!"

"Honah to 'is name!" concorded Aunt Rachel. "Wuthy all praise! Tang God fah wat I seen an' heahn dis night! dis night long to be membed! Meh soul feels it! It is heah!" pressing her hand upon her breast, exclaimed she.

"Amen! Laud heah de cry uh dy children! Anseh prah!" responded the old man, in tears; when Aunt Rachel in a grain of sorrowful pathos, sung to the expressive words in the slaves' lament:

> "In eighteen hundred and twenty-three
> They said their people should be free!
> It is wrote in Jeremiah,
> Come and go along with me!
> It is wrote in Jeremiah,
> Go sound the Jubilee!"

At the conclusion of the last line, a sudden sharp rap at the door startled them, when the old woman, hastening, took down the quilt, enquiring, "Who dat?"

"Open the door, Rachel!" was the reply, in an authoritative tone from a posse of patrols, who on going their evening rounds were attracted to the place by the old people's devotion, and stood sometime listening around the hut.

"You seem to be happy here, Jerry," said Ralph Jordon, the head of the party. "What boy is this you have here?"

"Major Morgan's sir," replied Henry, referring to the proprietor of the next plantation above.

"I don't remember seeing you before, boy," continued Jordon.

"No, sir; lately got me," explained Henry.

"Aye, aye, boy; a preacher, I suppose."

"No, sir."

"No, Maus Rafe, dis brotheh no preacheh; but 'e is 'logious, and come to gib us little comfit, an' bless God I feels it now; dat I does, blessed be God!" said the old woman.

"Well, Rachel, that's all right enough; but, my boy, its high time that you were getting towards home. You've not learned our rules here; where are you from?"

"Louisiana, sir."

"Yes, yes, that explains it. Louisiana Negroes are permitted to go out at a much later hour than our Negroes."

"Maus Rafe, ah hope yah let de brotheh eat a mouph'l wid us fo' go?"

"O yes, Rachel! give the boy something to eat before he goes; I suppose the 'laborer is worthy of his hire,'" looking with a smile at his comrades.

"Yes 'ndeed, seh, dat he is!" replied the old woman with emphasis.

"Rachel, I smell something good! What have you here, spare rib?" enquired Ralph Jordon, walking to the table and lifting up a clean check apron which the old woman had hurriedly thrown over it to screen her homely food from the view of the gentlemen patrols. "Good! spare rib and ash cake, gentlemen! What's better? Rachel, give us some seats here!" continued Ralph.

Hurrying about, the old woman made out to seat the uninvited guests with a half barrel tub, an old split bottom chair, and a short slab bench, which accommodated two.

"By gum! This is fine," said Ralph Jordon, smacking his mouth, and tearing at a rib. "Gentlemen, help yourselves to some spirits," setting on the table a large flask of Jamaica rum, just taken from his lips.

"Nothing better," replied Tom Hammond; "give me at any time the cooking in the Negro quarters before your great-house dainties."

"So say I," sanctioned Zack Hite, champing like a hungry man. "The Negroes live a great deal better than we do."

"Much better, sir, much better," replied Ralph. "Rachel, don't you nor Jerry ever take any spirits?"

"No, Maus Rafe, not any," replied the old woman.

"May be your friend there will take a little."

"I don't drink, sir," said Henry.

Rising from the homely meal at the humble board of Aunt Rachel and Uncle Jerry, they emptied their pockets of crackers, cold biscuits and cheese, giving the old man a plug of honey-cured tobacco, to be divided between himself and wife, in lieu of what they had, without invitation, taken the liberty of eating. The patrol this evening were composed of the better class of persons, principally business men, two of whom, being lawyers who went out that evening for a mere "frolic among the Negroes."

Receiving the parting hand, accompanied with a "good bye, honey!" and "God bless yeh, meh son!" from the old people, Henry left the hut to continue his course through the forest. Hearing persons approaching, he stepped aside from the road to conceal himself, when two parties at the junction of two roads met each other, coming to a stand.

"What's up tonight, Colonel?" enquired one.

"Nothing but the raffle."

"Are you going?"

"Yes, the whole party here; won't you go?"

"I dun'o; what's the chances?"

"Five dollars only."

"Five dollars a chance! What the deuce is the prize!"

"Oh, there's several for the same money."

"What are they?"

"That fine horse and buggy of Colonel Sprout, a mare and colt, a little Negro girl ten years of age, and a trail of four of the finest Negro-dogs in the state."

"Hallo! all them; why, how many chances, in the name of gracious, are there?"

"Only a hundred and fifty."

"Seven hundred and fifty dollars for the whole; that's cheap. But, then, all can't win, and it must be a loss to somebody."

"Will you go, Cap'n?"

"Well, I don't care—go it is!" when the parties started in the direction of the sport, Henry following to reconnoiter them.

On approaching the tavern, the rafflers, who waited the rest of the company to gather, could be seen and heard through the uncurtained windows and the door, which was frequently opened, standing around a blazing hot fire, and in groups over the barroom floor, amusing themselves with jests and laughter. Henry stood in the verge of the forest in a position to view the whole of their proceedings.

Presently there was a rush out of doors with glee and merriment. Old Colonel Sprout was bringing out his dogs, to test their quality previous to the raffle.

"Now, gentlemen!" exclaimed he, "them is the best trained dogs in this part of the state. Be dad, they's the bes' dogs in the country. When you say 'nigger,' you needn't fear they'll ever go after anything but a nigger."

"Come, Colonel, give them a trial; we must have something going on to kill time," suggested one of the party.

"But what will he try 'em on?" said another; "there's no niggers to hunt."

"Send them out, and let them find one, be George; what else would you have them do?" replied a third.

"Where the deuce will they get one?" rejoined a fourth.

"Just as a hunting dog finds any other game," answered a fifth; "where else?"

"O, by golly, gentlemen, you need's give yourselves no uneasiness about the game. They'll find a nigger, once started if they have to break into some Negro quarter and drag 'm out o' bed. No mistake 'bout them, I tell you, gentlemen," boasted Sprout.

"But won't a nigger hurt 'em when he knows he's not a runaway?" enquired Richard Rester Rutherford.

"What, a nigger hurt a bloodhound! By, gracious, they're fearder of a bloodhound than they is of the devil himself! Them dogs is dogs, gentlemen, an' no mistake; they is by gracious!" declared Sprout.

"Well, let them loose, Colonel, and let's have a little sport, at any rate!" said Ralph Jordon, the patrol, who had just arrived; "we're in for a spree tonight, anyhow."

"Here, Caesar, Major, Jowler, here Pup! Niggers about! Seek out!" hissed the Colonel, with a snap of the finger, pointing toward the thicket, in the direction of which was Henry. With a yelp which sent a shudder through the crowd, the dogs started in full chase for the forest.

"By George, Colonel, that's too bad! Call them back!" said Ralph Jordon, as the savage brutes bounded in search of a victim.

"By thunder, gentlemen, it's too late! they'll have a nigger before they stop. They'll taste the blood of some poor black devil before they git back!" declared Sprout.

Having heard every word that passed between them, in breathless silence Henry waited the approach of the animals. The yelping now became more anxious and eager, until at last it was heard as a short, impatient, fretful whining, indicating a near approach to their prey, when growing less and less, they ceased entirely to be heard.

"What the Harry does it mean! the dogs has ceased to bay!" remarked Colonel Sprout.

"Maybe they caught a nigger," replied John Spangler.

"It might be a Tartar!" rejoined Ralph Jordon.

"Maybe a nigger caught them!" said the Sheriff of the county, who was present to superintend the raffle, and receive the proceeds of the hazard.

"What!" exclaimed the old gentleman, to enhance the value of the prizes. "What! My Caesar, Major, Jowler, and Pup, the best dogs in all Arkansas!—A nigger kill them! No, gentlemen, once let loose an' on their trail, an' they's not a gang o' niggers to be found out at night they couldn't devour! Them dogs! Hanged if they didn't eat a nigger quicker as they'd swaller a piece o' meat!"

"Then they're the dogs for me!" replied the Sheriff.

"And me," added Spangle, a noted agent for catching runaway slaves.

"The raffle, the raffle!" exclaimed several voices eager for a chance, estimating at once the value of the dogs above the aggregate amount of the stakes.

"But the dogs, the dogs, gentlemen! They're not here! Give us the dogs first," suggested an eager candidate for competition in the prizes.

"No matter, gentlemen; be sartin," said the Colonel, "when they's done they'll come back agin."

"But how will they be managed in attacking strange Negroes?" enquired Ralph Jordon.

"O, the command of any white man is sufficient to call 'em off, an' they's plenty o' them all'as wherever you find niggers."

"Then, Colonel, we're to understand you to mean, that white men can't live without niggers."

"I'll be hanged, gentlemen, if it don't seem so, for wherever you find one you'll all'as find tother, they's so fully mixed up with us in all our relations!" peals of laughter following the explanation.

MARTIN R. DELANY

"Come, Colonel, I'll be hanged if we stand that, except you stand treat!" said Ralph.

"Stand what? Let us understand you; what'd I say?"

"What did you say? why, by George, you tell us flatly that we are related to niggers!"

"Then, gentlemen, I'll stand treat; for on that question I'll be consarned if some of us don't have to knock under!" at which there were deafening roars of laughter, the crowd rushing into the barroom, crying, "Treat! Treat!! That's too good to be lost!"

Next day after the raffle, the winners having presented the prizes back to their former owner, it was whispered about that the dogs had been found dead in the woods, the mare and colt were astray, the little slave girl was in a pulmonary decline, the buggy had been upset and badly worsted the day before the raffle, and the horse had the distemper; upon which information the whole party met at a convenient place on a fixed day, going out to his house in a body, who ate, drank, and caroused at his expense during the day and evening.

"Sprout," said Ralph Jordon, "with your uniform benevolence, generosity and candor, how did you ever manage to depart so far from your old principles and rule of doing things? I can't understand it."

"How so? Explain yourself," replied Sprout.

"Why you always give rather than take advantage, your house and means always being open to the needy, even those with whom you are unacquainted."

"I'm sure I ain't departed one whit from my old rule," said Sprout; "I saw you was all strangers to the thing, an' I took you in; I'm blamed if I didn't!" the crowd shouting with laughter.

"One word, Sprout," said Jordon. "When the dogs ceased baying, didn't you suspect something wrong?"

"I know'd at once when they stopped that they was defeated; but I thought they'd pitched headlong into a old wellhole some sixty foot deep, where the walls has tumbled in, an' made it some twenty foot wide at the top. I lis'ened every minute 'spectin' to hear a devil of a whinin' 'mong 'em' but I was disapinted."

"Well, its a blamed pity, anyhow, that such fine animals were killed; and no clue as yet, I believe, to the perpetration of the deed," said the Sheriff.

"They was, indeed," replied Sprout, "as good a breed o' dogs as ever was, an' if they'd a been trained right, nothin' could a come up with them; but consarn their picters, it serves 'em right, as they wos the cussedest cowards I ever seed! 'Sarn them, if a nigger ony done so—jis' made a pass at 'em, an' I'll be hanged if they didn't yelp like wild cats, an almost kill 'emselves runin' away!" at which explanation the peals of laughter were deafening.

"Let's stay a week, stay a week, gentlemen!" exclaimed Ralph Jordon, in a convulsion of laughter.

"Be gracious, gentlemen!" concluded Sprout. "If you stay till eternity it won't alter the case one whit; case, the mare an' colt's lost, the black gal's no use to anybody, the buggy's all smashed up, the hos' is got the distemper, and the dogs is dead as thunder!"

With a boisterous roar, the party, already nearly exhausted with laughter, commenced gathering their hats and cloaks, and left the premises declaring never again to be caught at a raffling wherein was interested Colonel Joel Sprout.

The dogs were the best animals of the kind, and quickly trailed out their game; but Henry, with a well-aimed weapon, slew each ferocious beast as it approached him, leaving them weltering in their own blood instead of feasting on his, as would have been the case had he not overpowered them. The rest of the prizes were also valuable and in good order, and the story which found currency depreciating them, had its origin in the brain and interest of Colonel Sprout, which resulted, as designed, entirely in his favor.

Hastening on to the Fulton landing Henry reached it at half-past two o'clock in the morning, just in time to board a steamer on the downward trip, which barely touched the shore to pick up a package. Knowing him by reputation as a great horse master, the captain received him cheerfully, believing him to have been, from what he had learned, to the Texas races with horses for his master.

Being now at ease, and faring upon the best the vessel could afford, after a little delay along the cotton trading coast, Henry was safely landed in the portentous city of New Orleans.

Chapter 22

New Orleans

The season is the holidays, it is evening, and the night is beautiful. The moon, which in Louisiana is always an object of impressive interest, even to the slave as well as those of enlightened and scientific intelligence, the influence of whose soft and mellow light seems ever like the enchanting effect of some invisible being, to impart inspiration—now being shed from the crescent of the first day of the last quarter, appeared more interesting and charming than ever.

Though the cannon at the old fort in the Lower Faubourg had fired the significant warning, admonishing the slaves as well as free blacks to limit their movement, still there were passing to and fro with seeming indifference Negroes, both free and slaves, as well as the whites and Creole quadroons, fearlessly along the public highways, in seeming defiance of the established usage of Negro limitation.

This was the evening of the day of Mardi Gras, and from long-established and time-honored custom, the celebration which commenced in the morning was now being consummated by games, shows, exhibitions, theatrical performances, festivals, masquerade balls, and numerous entertainments and gatherings in the evening. It was on this account that the Negroes had been allowed such unlimited privileges this evening.

Nor were they remiss to the utmost extent of its advantages.

The city which always at this season of the year is lively, and Chartier street gay and fashionable, at this time appeared more lively, gay and fashionable than usual. This fashionable thoroughfare, the pride of the city, was thronged with people, presenting complexions of every shade and color. Now could be seen and realized the expressive description in the popular song of the vocalist Cargill:

> *I suppose you've heard how New Orleans*
> *Is famed for wealth and beauty;*
> *There's girls of every hue, it seems,*
> *From snowy white to sooty.*

The extensive shops and fancy stores presented the presence behind their counters as saleswomen in attendance of numerous females, black, white, mulatto and quadroon, politely bowing, curtsying, and rubbing their hands, in accents of broken English inviting to purchase all who enter the threshold, or even look in at the door:

"Wat fa you want something? Walk in, sire, I vill sell you one nice present fa one young lady."

And so with many who stood or sat along the streets and at the store doors, curtsying and smiling they give the civil banter:

"Come, sire, I sell you one pretty ting."

The fancy stores and toy shops on this occasion were crowded seemingly to their greatest capacity. Here might be seen the fashionable young white lady of French or American extraction, and there the handsome, and frequently beautiful maiden of African origin, mulatto, quadroon, or sterling black, all fondly interchanging civilities, and receiving some memento or keepsake from the hand of an acquaintance. Many lively jests and impressive flings of delicate civility noted the greetings of the passersby. Freedom seemed as though for once enshielded by her sacred robes and crowned with cap and wand in hand, to go forth untrammeled through the highways of the town. Along the private streets, sitting under the verandas, in the doors with half-closed jalousies, or promenading unconcernedly the public ways, mournfully humming in solace or chanting in lively

glee, could be seen and heard many a Creole, male or female, black, white or mixed race, sometimes in reverential praise of

Father, Son and Holy Ghost—
Madonna, and the Heavenly Host!

in sentimental reflection on some pleasant social relations, or the sad reminiscence of ill-treatment or loss by death of some loved one, or worse than death, the relentless and insatiable demands of slavery.

In the distance, on the levee or in the harbor among the steamers, the songs of the boatmen were incessant. Every few hours landing, loading and unloading, the glee of these men of sorrow was touchingly appropriate and impressive. Men of sorrow they are in reality; for if there be a class of men anywhere to be found, whose sentiments of song and words of lament are made to reach the sympathies of others, the black slave-boatmen of the Mississippi river is that class. Placed in positions the most favorable to witness the pleasures enjoyed by others, the tendency is only to augment their own wretchedness.

Fastened by the unyielding links of the iron cable of despotism, reconciling themselves to a lifelong misery, they are seemingly contented by soothing their sorrows with songs and sentiments of apparently cheerful but in reality wailing lamentations. The most attracting lament of the evening was sung to words, a stanza of which is presented in pathos of delicate tenderness, which is but a spray from the stream which gushed out in insuppressible jets from the agitated fountains of their souls, as if in unison with the restless current of the great river upon which they were compelled to toil, their troubled waters could not be quieted. In the capacity of leader, as is their custom, one poor fellow in pitiful tones led off the song of the evening:

> *Way down upon the Mobile river,*
> *Close to Mobile bay;*
> *There's where my thoughts is running ever,*
> *All through the livelong day:*
> *There I've a good and fond old mother,*
> *Though she is a slave;*

> *There I've a sister and a brother,*
> *Lying in their peaceful graves.*

Then in chorus joined the whole company—

> *O, could I somehow a'nother,*
> *Drive these tears way;*
> *When I think about my poor old mother,*
> *Down upon the Mobile bay.*

Standing in the midst of and contemplating such scenes as these, it was that Henry determined to finish his mission in the city and leave it by the earliest conveyance over Pontchartrain for Alabama—Mobile being the point at which he aimed. Swiftly as the current of the fleeting Mississippi was time passing by, and many states lay in expanse before him, all of which, by the admonishing impulses of the dearest relations, he was compelled to pass over as a messenger of light and destruction.

Light, of necessity, had to be imparted to the darkened region of the obscure intellects of the slaves, to arouse them from their benighted condition to one of moral responsibility, to make them sensible that liberty was legitimately and essentially theirs, without which there was no distinction between them and the brute. Following as a necessary consequence would be the destruction of oppression and ignorance.

Alone and friendless, without a home, a fugitive from slavery, a child of misfortune and outcast upon the world, floating on the cold surface of chance, now in the midst of a great city of opulence, surrounded by the most despotic restrictions upon his race, with renewed determination Henry declared that nothing short of an unforeseen Providence should impede his progress in the spread of secret organization among the slaves. So aroused, he immediately started for a house in the Lower Faubourg.

"My frien', who yeh lookin' foh?" kindly enquired a cautious black man, standing concealed in the shrubbery near the door of a low, tile-covered house standing back in the yard.

"A friend," replied Henry.

"Wat's 'is name?" continued the man.

"I do not rightly know."

"Would yeh know it ef yeh heahed it, my fren'?"

"I think I would."

"Is it Seth?"

"That's the very name!" said Henry.

"Wat yeh want wid 'im, my fren'?"

"I want to see him."

"I spose yeh do, fren'; but dat ain' answer my questin' yet. Wat yeh want wid 'em?"

"I would rather see him, then I'll be better able to answer."

"My fren'," replied the man, meaningly, "ah see da is somethin' in yeh; come in!" giving a significant cough before placing his finger on the latchstring.

On entering, from the number and arrangement of the seats, there was evidence of an anticipated gathering; but the evening being that of the Mardi Gras, there was nothing remarkable in this. Out from another room came a sharp, observing, shrewd little dark brown-skin woman, called in that community a griffe. Bowing, sidling and curtsying, she smilingly came forward.

"Wat brotha dis, Seth?" enquired she.

"Ah don'o," carelessly replied he with a signal of caution, which was not required in her case.

"Ah!" exclaimed Henry. "This is Mr. Seth! I'm glad to see you."

After a little conversation, in which freely participated Mrs. Seth, who evidently was deservingly the leading spirit of the evening, they soon became reconciled to the character and mission of their unexpected and self-invited guest.

"Phebe, go tell 'em," said Seth; when lightly tripping away she entered the door of the other room, which after a few moments' delay was partially opened, and by a singular and peculiar signal, Seth and the stranger were invited in. Here sat in one of the most secret and romantic-looking rooms, a party of fifteen, the representatives of the heads of that many plantations, who that night had gathered for the portentious purpose of a final decision on the hour to strike the first blow. On entering, Henry stood a little in check.

"Trus' 'em!" said Seth. "Yeh fine 'em da right saut uh boys—true to deh own color! Da come fom fifteen diffent plantation."

"They're the men for me!" replied Henry, looking around the room. "Is the house all safe?"

"Yes brotha, all safe an' soun', an' a big dog in da yahd, so dat no one can come neah widout ouah knowin' it."

"First, then, to prayer, and next to seclusion," said Henry, looking at Seth to lead in prayer.

"Brotha, gib us wud a' prah," said Seth to Henry, as the party on their knees bowed low their heads to the floor.

"I am not fit, brother, for a spiritual leader; my warfare is not Heavenly, but earthly; I have not to do with angels, but with men; not with righteousness, but wickedness. Call upon some brother who has more of the grace of God than I. If I ever were a Christian, slavery has made me a sinner; if I had been an angel, it would have made me a devil! I feel more like cursing than praying—may God forgive me! Pray for me, brethren!"

"Brotha Kits, gib us wud a prah, my brotha!" said Seth to an athletic, powerful black man.

"Its not fah ouah many wuds, noah long prah—ouah 'pinion uh ouah self, nah sich like, dat Dou anseh us; but de 'cerity ob ouah hahts an ouah 'tentions. Bless de young man dat come 'mong us; make 'im fit fah 'is day, time, an' genration! Dou knows, Laud, dat fah wat we 'semble; anseh dis ouah 'tition, an' gib us token ob Dine 'probation!" petitioned

Kits, slapping his hand at the conclusion down upon and splitting open a pine table before him.

"Amen," responded the gathering.

"Let da wud run an' be glorify!" exclaimed Nathan Seth.

The splitting of the table was regarded as ominous, but of doubtful signification, the major part considering it as rather unfavorable. Making no delay, lest a despondency ensue through fear and superstition, Henry at once entered into seclusion, completing an organization.

"God sen' yeh had come along dis way befo'!" exclaimed Phebe Seth.

"God grant 'e had!" responded Nathan.

"My Laud! I feels like a Sampson! ah feels like gwine up to take de city mehself!" cried out Kits, standing erect in the floor with fists clenched, muscles braced, eyes shut, and head thrown back.

"Yes, yes!" exclaimed Phebe. "Blessed be God, brotha Kits, da King is in da camp!"

"Powah, powah!" responded Seth. "Da King is heah!"

"Praise 'is name!" shouted Phebe clapping and rubbing her hands. "Fah wat I feels an' da knowledge I has receive dis night! I been all my days in darkness till now! I feels we shall be a people yit! Thang' God, thang God!" when she skidded over the floor from side to side, keeping time with a tune sung to the words—

> "We'll honor our Lord and Master;
> We'll honor our Lord and King;
> We'll honor our Lord and Master,
> And bow at His command!
> O! brothers, did you hear the news?
> Lovely Jesus is coming!
> If ever I get to the house of the Lord,
> I'll never come back any more."

"It's good to be heah!" shouted Seth.

"Ah! dat it is, brotha Seth!" responded Kits. "Da Laud is nigh, dat 'e is! 'e promise whahsomeveh two-three 'semble, to be in da mids' and dat to bless 'em, an' 'is promise not in vain, case 'e heah tonight!"

At the moment which Phebe took her seat, nearly exhausted with exercise, a loud rap at the door, preceded by the signal for the evening, alarmed the party.

"Come in, brotha Tib—come quick, if yeh comin!" bade Seth, in a low voice hastily, as he partially opened the door, peeping out into the other room.

"O, pshaw!" exclaimed Phebe, as she and her husband yet whispered; "I wish he stay away. I sho nobody want 'em! he all'as half drunk anyhow. Good ev'nin', brotha Tib. How yeh been sense we see yeh early paut da night?"

"Reasable, sistah—reasable, thang God. Well, what yeh all 'cided on? I say dis night now au neveh!" said Tib, evidently bent on mischief.

"Foolishness, foolishness!" replied Phebe. "It make me mad see people make fool uh demself! I wish 'e stay home an' not bothen heah!"

"Ah, 'spose I got right to speak as well as da rest on yeh! Yeh all ain' dat high yit to keep body fom talkin', ah 'spose. Betta wait tell yeh git free fo' ye 'temp' scrow oveh people dat way! I kin go out yeh house!" retorted the mischievous man, determined on distracting their plans.

"Nobody odeh yeh out, but I like see people have sense, specially befo' strangehs! an' know how behave demself!"

"I is gwine out yeh house," gruffly replied the man.

"My friend," said Henry, "listen a moment to me. You are not yet ready for a strike; you are not yet ready to do anything effective. You have barely taken the first step in the matter, and—"

"Strangeh!" interrupted the distracter. "Ah don'o yeh name, yeh strangeh to me—I see yeh talk 'bout 'step'; how many step man got take fo' 'e kin walk? I likes to know dat! Tell me that fus, den yeh may ax me what yeh choose!"

"You must have all the necessary means, my brother," persuasively resumed Henry, "for the accomplishment of your ends. Intelligence among yourself on everything pertaining to your designs and project. You must know what, how, and when to do. Have all the instrumentalities necessary for an effective effort, before making the attempt. Without this, you will fail, utterly fail!"

"Den ef we got wait all dat time, we neveh be free!" gruffly replied he. "I goes in foh dis night! I say dis night! Who goes—"

"Shet yo' big mouth! Sit down! Now make a fool o' yo'self!" exclaimed several voices with impatience, which evidently only tended to increase the mischief.

"Dis night, dis night au neveh!" boisterously yelled the now infuriated man at the top of his voice. "Now's da time!" when he commenced shuffling about over the floor, stamping and singing at the top of his voice—

Come all my brethren, let us take a rest,
While the moon shines bright and clear;
Old master died and left us all at last,
And has gone at the bar to appear!
Old master's dead and lying in his grave;
And our blood will now cease to flow;
He will no more tramp on the neck of the slave,
For he's gone where slaveholders go!
Hang up the shovel and the hoe—o—o—o!
I don't care whether I work or no!

Old master's gone to the slaveholders rest—
He's gone where they all ought to go!

pointing down and concluding with an expression which indicated anything but a religious feeling.

"Shame so it is dat he's 'lowed to do so! I wish I was man foh 'im, I'd make 'im fly!" said Phebe much alarmed, as she heard the great dog in the yard, which had been so trained as to know the family visitors, whining and manifesting an uneasiness unusual with him. On going to the back door, a person suddenly retreated into the shrubbery, jumping the fence, and disappearing.

Soon, however, there was an angry low heavy growling of the dog, with suppressed efforts to bark, apparently prevented by fear on the part of the animal. This was succeeded by cracking in the bushes, dull heavy footsteps, cautious whispering, and stillness.

"Hush! Listen!" admonished Phebe. "What is dat? Wy don't Tyger bark? I don't understan' it! Seth, go out and see, will you? Wy don't some you men make dat fool stop? I wish I was man, I'd break 'is neck, so I would!" during which the betrayer was shuffling, dancing, and singing at such a pitch as to attract attention from without.

Seth seizing him from behind by a firm grasp of the collar with both hands, Tib sprang forward, slipping easily out of it, leaving the overcoat suspended in his assailant's hands, displaying studded around his waist a formidable array of deathly weapons, when rushing out of the front door, he in terrible accents exclaimed—

"Insurrection! Insurrection! Death to every white!"

With a sudden spring of their rattles, the gendarmes, who in cloisters had surrounded the house, and by constant menacing gestures with their maces kept the great dog, which stood back in a corner, in a snarling position in fear, arrested the miscreant, taking him directly to the old fort calaboose. In the midst of the confusion which necessarily ensued, Henry, Seth, and Phebe, Kits and fellow-leaders from the fifteen plantations, immediately fled, all having passes for the day and evening, which fully protected them in any part of the city away from the scene of disturbance.

Intelligence soon reached all parts of the city, that an extensive plot for rebellion of the slaves had been timely detected. The place was at once thrown into a state of intense excitement, the military called into requisition, dragoons flying in every direction, cannon from the old fort sending forth hourly through the night, thundering peals to give assurance of their sufficiency, and the infantry on duty traversing the streets, stimulating with martial air with voluntary vocalists, who readily joined in chorus to the memorable citing words in the Southern States of—Go tell Jack Coleman, The Negroes are arising!

Alarm and consternation succeeded pleasure and repose, sleep for the time seemed to have departed from the eyes of the inhabitants, men, women and children ran every direction through the streets, seeming determined if they were to be massacred, that it should be done in the open highways rather than secretly in their own houses. The commotion thus continued till the morning; meanwhile editors, journalists, reporters, and correspondents, all were busily on the alert, digesting such information as would form an item of news for the press, or a standing reminiscence for historical reference in the future.

Chapter 23

The Rebel Blacks

For the remainder of the night secreting themselves in Conti and Burgundi streets, the rebel proprietors of the house in which was laid the plot for the destruction of the city were safe until the morning, their insurrectionary companions having effected a safe retreat to the respective plantations to which they belonged that evening.

Jason and Phebe Seth were the hired slaves of their own time from a widower master, a wealthy retired attorney at Baton Rouge, whose only concern about them was to call every ninety days at the counter of the Canal Bank of New Orleans, and receive the price of their hire, which was there safely deposited to his credit by the industrious and faithful servants. The house in which the rebels met had been hired for the occasion, being furnished rooms kept for transient accommodation.

On the earliest conveyance destined for the City of Mobile, Henry left, who, before he fled, admonished as his parting counsel, to "stand still and see the salvation"; the next day being noted by General Ransom, as an incident in his history, to receive a formal visit of a fortnight's sojourn, in the person of his slaves Jason and Phebe Seth.

The inquisition held in the case of the betrayer Tib developed fearful antecedents of extensive arrangements for the destruction of the city by fire and water, thereby compelling the white inhabitants to take refuge in the swamps, whilst the blacks marched up the coast, sweeping the plantations as they went.

Suspicions were fixed upon many, among whom was an unfortunate English schoolteacher, who was arrested and imprisoned, when he died, to the last protesting his innocence. Mr. Farland was a good and bravehearted man, disdaining to appeal for redress to his country, lest it might be regarded as the result of cowardice.

Taking fresh alarm at this incident, the municipal regulations have been most rigid in a system of restriction and espionage toward Negroes and mulattoes, almost destroying their self-respect and manhood, and certainly impairing their usefulness.

Chapter 24

A Flying Cloud

S afely in Mobile Henry landed without a question, having on the way purchased of a passenger who was deficient of means to bear expenses, a horse by which he made a daring entry into the place. Mounting the animal which was fully caparisoned, he boldly rode to the principal livery establishment, ordering for it the greatest care until his master's arrival.

Hastening into the country he readily found a friend and seclusion in the hut of Uncle Cesar, on the plantation of Gen. Audly. Making no delay, early next morning he returned to the city to effect a special object. Passing by the stable where the horse had been left, a voice loudly cried out:

"There's that Negro boy, now! Hallo, there, boy! didn't you leave a horse here?"

Heeding not the interrogation, but speedily turning the first corner, Henry hastened away and was soon lost among the inhabitants.

"How yeh do, me frien'?" saluted a black man whom he met in a by-street. "Ar' yeh strangeh?"

"Why?" enquired Henry.

"O, nothin'! On'y I hearn some wite men talkin'j's now, an' da say some strange nigga lef' a hoss dar, an' da blev 'e stole 'em, an' da gwine ketch an' put 'em in de jail."

"If that's all, I live here. Good morning!" rejoined he who soon was making rapid strides in the direction of Georgia.

Every evening found him among the quarters of some plantations, safely secreted in the hut of some faithful, trustworthy slave, with attentive, anxious listeners, ready for an issue. So, on he went with flying haste, from plantation to plantation, till Alabama was left behind him.

In Georgia, though the laws were strict, the Negroes were equally hopeful. Like the old stock of Maryland and Virginia blacks from whom they were descended, they manifested a high degree of intelligence for slaves. Receiving their messenger with open arms, the aim of his advent among them spread like fire in a stubble. Everywhere seclusions were held and organizations completed, till Georgia stands like a city at the base of a burning mountain, threatened with destruction by an overflow of the first outburst of lava from above. Clearing the state without an obstruction, he entered that which of all he most dreaded, the haughty South Carolina.

Here the most relentless hatred appears to exist against the Negro, who seems to be regarded but as an animated thing of convenience or a domesticated animal, reared for the service of his master. The studied policy of the whites evidently is to keep the blacks in subjection and their spirits below a sentiment of self-respect. To impress the Negro with a sense of his own inferiority is a leading precept of their social system; to be white is the only evidence necessary to establish a claim to superiority. To be a "master" in South Carolina is to hold a position of rank and title, and he who approaches this the nearest is heightened at least in his own estimation.

These feelings engendered by the whites have been extensively incorporated with the elements of society among the colored people, giving rise to the "Brown Society" an organized association of mulattos, created by the influence of the whites, for the purpose of preventing pure-blooded Negroes from entering the social circle, or holding intercourse with them.

Here intelligence and virtue are discarded and ignored, when not in conformity with these regulations. A man with the prowess of Memnon, or a woman with the purity of the "black doves" of Ethiopia and charms of the "black virgin" of Solomon, avails them nothing, if the blood of the oppressor, engendered by wrong, predominates not in their veins.

Oppression is the author of all this, and upon the heads of the white masters let the terrible responsibility of this miserable stupidity and ignorance of their mulatto children rest; since to them was left the plan of their social salvation, let upon their consciences rest the penalties of their social damnation.

The transit of the runaway through this state was exceedingly difficult, as no fabrication of which he was capable could save him from the penalties of arrest. To assume freedom would be at once to consign himself to endless bondage, and to acknowledge himself a slave was at once to advertise for a master. His only course of safety was to sleep through the day and travel by night, always keeping to the woods.

At a time just at the peep of day when making rapid strides the baying of hounds and soundings of horns were heard at a distance.

Understanding it to be the sport of the chase, Henry made a hasty retreat to the nearest hiding place which presented, in the hollow of a log. On attempting to creep in a snarl startled him, when out leaped the fox, having counterrun his track several times, and sheltered in a fallen sycamore. Using his remedy for distracting dogs, he succeeded the fox in the sycamore, resting in safety during the day without molestation, though the dogs bayed within thirty yards of him, taking a contrary course by the distraction of their scent.

For every night of sojourn in the state he had a gathering, not one of which was within a hut, so closely were the slaves watched by patrol, and sometimes by mulatto and black overseers. These gatherings were always held in the forest. Many of the confidants of the seclusions were the much-dreaded runaways of the woods, a class of outlawed slaves, who continually seek the lives of their masters.

One day having again sought retreat in a hollow log where he lay sound asleep, the day being chilly, he was awakened by a cold application to his face and neck, which proved to have been made by a rattlesnake of the largest size, having sought the warmth of his bosom.

HENRY MADE A HASTY RETREAT, ever after declining the hollow of a tree. With rapid movements and hasty action, he like a wind cloud flew through the State of South Carolina, who like "a thief in the night" came when least expected.

Henry now entered Charleston, the metropolis, and head of the "Brown Society," the bane and dread of the blacks in the state, an organization formed through the instrumentality of the whites to keep the blacks and mulattos at variance. To such an extent is the error carried, that the members of the association, rather than their freedom would prefer to see the blacks remain in bondage. But many most excellent mulattos and quadroons condemn with execration this auxiliary of oppression. The eye of the intelligent world is on this "Brown Society"; and its members when and wherever seen are scanned with suspicion and distrust. May they not be forgiven for their ignorance when proving by repentance their conviction of wrong?

Lying by till late next morning, he entered the city in daylight, having determined boldly to pass through the street, as he might not be known from any common Negro. Coming to an extensive wood-yard he learned by an old black man who sat at the gate that the proprietors were two colored men, one of whom he pointed out, saying:

"Dat is my mausta."

Approaching a respectable-looking mulatto gentleman standing in conversation with a white, his foot resting on a log:

"Do you wish to hire help, sir?" enquired Henry respectfully touching his cap.

"Take off your hat, boy!" ordered the mulatto gentleman. Obeying the order, he repeated the question.

"Who do you belong to?" enquired the gentleman.

"I am free, sir!" replied he.

"You are a free boy? Are you not a stranger here?"

"Yes, sir."

"Then you lie, sir," replied the mulatto gentleman, "as you know that no free Negro is permitted to enter this state. You are a runaway, and I'll have you taken up!" at the same time walking through his office looking out at the front door as if for an officer.

Making a hasty retreat, in less than an hour he had left the city, having but a few minutes tarried in the hut of an old black family on the suburb, one of the remaining confidentials and adherents of the memorable South Carolina insurrection, when and to whom he imparted his fearful scheme.

"Ah!" said the old man, throwing his head in the lap of his old wife, with his hands around her neck, both of whom sat near the chimney with the tears coursing down their furrowed cheeks. "Dis many a day I been prayin' dat de Laud sen' a nudder Denmark 'mong us! De Laud now anseh my prar in dis young man! Go on, my son—go on—an' may God A'mighty bress yeh!"

North Carolina was traversed mainly in the night. When approaching the region of the Dismal Swamp, a number of the old confederates of the noted Nat Turner were met with, who hailed the daring young runaway as the harbinger of better days. Many of these are still long-suffering, hard-laboring slaves on the plantations; and some bold, courageous, and fearless adventurers, denizens of the mystical, antiquated, and almost fabulous Dismal Swamp, where for many years they have defied the approach of their pursuers.

Here Henry found himself surrounded by a different atmosphere, an entirely new element. Finding ample scope for undisturbed action through the entire region of the Swamp, he continued to go scattering to the winds and sowing the seeds of a future crop, only to take root in the thick black waters which cover it, to be grown in devastation and reaped in a whirlwind of ruin.

"I been lookin' fah yeh dis many years," said old Gamby Gholar, a noted high conjurer and compeer of Nat Turner, who for more than thirty years has been secluded in the Swamp, "an' been tellin' on 'em dat yeh 'ood come long, but da 'ooden' heah dat I tole 'em! Now da see! Dis many years I been seein' on yeh! Yes, 'ndeed, chile, dat I has!" and he took from a gourd of antiquated appearance which hung against the wall in his hut, many articles of a mysterious character, some resembling bits of woollen yarn, onionskins, oystershells, finger and toenails, eggshells, and scales which he declared to be from very dangerous serpents, but which closely resembled, and were believed to be those of innocent and harmless fish, with broken iron nails.

These he turned over and over again in his hands, closely inspecting them through a fragment of green bottle glass, which he claimed to be a mysterious and precious "blue stone" got at a peculiar and unknown spot in the Swamp, whither by a special faith he was led—and ever after unable to find the same spot—putting them again into the gourd, the end of the neck being cut off so as to form a bottle, he rattled the "goombah," as he termed it, as if endeavoring to frighten his guest. This process ended, he whispered, then sighted into the neck, first with one eye, then with the other, then shook, and so alternately whispering, sighting and shaking, until apparently getting tired, again pouring them out, fumbling among them until finding a forked breast-bone of a small bird, which, muttering to himself, he called the "charm bone of a treefrog."

"Ah," exclaimed Gamby as he selected out the mystic symbol handing it to Henry, "got yeh at las'. Take dis, meh son, an' so long as yeh keep it, da can' haum yeh, dat da can't. Dis woth money, meh son; da ain't many sich like dat in de Swamp! Yeh never want for nothin' so long as yeh keep dat!"

In this fearful abode for years of some of Virginia and North Carolina's boldest black rebels, the names of Nat Turner, Denmark Veezie, and General Gabriel were held by them in sacred reverence; that of Gabriel as a talisman. With delight they recounted the many exploits of whom they conceived to be the greatest men who ever lived, the pretended deeds of whom were fabulous, some of the narrators claiming to have been patriots in the American Revolution.

"Yeh offen hearn on Maudy Ghamus," said an old man stooped with age, having the appearance of a centenarian. "Dat am me—me heah!" continued he, touching himself on the breast. "I's de frien' on Gamby Gholar; an' I an' Gennel Gabel fit in de Malution wah, an' da want no sich fightin' dare as dat in Gabel wah!"

"You were then a soldier in the Revolutionary War for American independence, father?" enquired Henry.

"Gau bress yeh, hunny. Yes, 'ndeed, chile, long 'for yeh baun; dat I did many long day go! Yes, chile, yes!"

"And General Gabriel, too, a soldier of the American Revolution?" replied Henry.

"Ah, chile, dat 'e did fit in de Molution wah, Gabel so, an' 'e fit like mad dog! Wen 'e sturt, chile, da can't stop 'im; da may as well let 'im go long, da can't do nuffin' wid 'im."

Henry subscribed to his eminent qualifications as a warrior, assuring him that those were the kind of fighting men they then needed among the blacks. Maudy Ghamus to this assented, stating that the Swamp contained them in sufficient number to take the whole United States; the only difficulty in the way being that the slaves in the different states could not be convinced of their strength. He had himself for years been an emissary; also, Gamby Gholar, who had gone out among them with sufficient charms to accomplish all they desired, but could not induce the slaves to a general rising.

"Take plenty goomba an' fongosa 'long wid us, an' plant mocasa all along, an' da got nuffin' fah do but come, an' da 'ooden come!" despairingly declared Maudy Ghamus.

Gamby Gholar, Maudy Ghamus, and others were High Conjurors, who as ambassadors from the Swamp, were regularly sent out to create new conjurers, lay charms, take off "spells" that could not be reached by Low Conjurors, and renew the art of all conjurors of seven years existence, at the expiration of which period the virtue was supposed to run out; holding their official position by fourteen years appointments. Through this means the revenue is obtained for keeping up an organized existence in this much-dreaded morass—the Dismal Swamp.

Before Henry left they insisted upon, and anointed him a priest of the order of High Conjurors, and amusing enough it was to him who consented to satisfy the aged devotees of a time-honored superstition among them. Their supreme executive body called the "Head" consists in number of seven aged men, noted for their superior experience and wisdom. Their place of official meeting must be entirely secluded, either in the forest, a gully, secluded hut, an underground room, or a cave.

The seven old men who, with heightened spirits, hailed his advent among them, led Henry to the door of an ample cave—their hollow— at the door of which they were met by a large sluggish, lazily-moving serpent, but so entirely tame and petted that it wagged its tail with fondness toward Maudy as he led the party. The old men, suddenly stopping at the approach of the reptile, stepping back a pace, looked at each other mysteriously shaking their heads:

"Go back!" exclaimed Maudy waving his hand. "Go back, my chile! 'e in terrible rage! 'e got seben long toof, any on 'em kill yeh like flash!" tapping it slightly on the head with a twig of grapevine which he carried in his hand.

Looking at the ugly beast, Henry had determined did it approach to harm, to slay it; but instead, it quietly coiled up and lay at the door as if asleep, which reminded him of queer and unmeaning sounds as they approached, uttered by Gholar, which explained that the animal had been trained to approach when called as any other pet. The "Head" once in session, they created him conjuror of the highest degree known to their art. With this qualification he was licensed with unlimited power—a power before given no one—to go forth and do wonders. The "Head" seemed, by the unlimited power given him, to place greater reliance in the efforts of Henry for their deliverance than in their own seven heads together.

"Go, my son," said they, "an' may God A'mighty hole up yo' han's an' grant us speedy 'liverence!"

Being now well refreshed—having rested without the fear of detection—and in the estimation of Gholar, Ghamus and the rest of the "Heads," well qualified to prosecute his project amidst the prayers, blessings, wishes, hopes, fears, pow-wows and promises of a never failing conjuration, and tears of the cloudy inhabitants of this great seclusion, among whom were the frosty-headed, bowed-down old men of the Cave, Henry left that region by his usual stealthy process, reaching Richmond, Virginia, in safety.

Chapter 25

LIKE FATHER, LIKE SON

With his usual adroitness, early in the morning, Henry entered Richmond boldly walking through the streets. This place in its municipal regulations, the customs and usages of society, the tastes and assumptive pride of the inhabitants, much resembles Charleston, South Carolina, the latter being a modified model of the former.

The restrictions here concerning Negroes and mulattos are less rigid, as they may be permitted to continue in social or religious gatherings after nine o'clock at night provided a white person be present to inspect their conduct; and may ride in a carriage, smoke a cigar in daylight, or walk with a staff at night.

According to an old-existing custom said to have originated by law, a mulatto or quadroon who proved a white mother were themselves regarded as white: and many availing themselves of the fact, took advantage of it by leaving their connections with the blacks and turning entirely over to the whites. Their children take further advantage of this by intermarrying with the whites, by which their identity becomes extinct, and they enter every position in society both social and political. Some of the proudest American statesmen in either House of the Capital, receive their poetic vigor of imagination from the current of Negro blood flowing in their veins.

Like those of Charleston, some of the light mixed bloods of Richmond hold against the blacks and pure-blooded Negroes the strongest prejudice and hatred, all engendered by the teachings of their Negro-fearing master-fathers. All of the terms and epithets of disparagement commonly used by the whites toward the blacks are as readily applied to them by this class of the mixed bloods. Shy of the blacks and fearful of the whites, they go sneaking about with the countenance of a criminal, of one conscious of having done wrong to his fellows. Spurned by the one and despised by the other, they are the least happy of all the classes. Of this class was Mrs. Pierce, whose daughter stood in the hall door, quite early enjoying the cool air this morning.

"Miss," enquired Henry of the young quadroon lady, "can you inform me where I'll find the house of Mr. Norton, a colored family in this city?" politely raising his cap as he approached her.

With a screech she retreated into the house, exclaiming, that a black Negro at the door had given her impudence. Startled at this alarm so unexpected to him—though somewhat prepared for such from his recent experience in Charleston—Henry made good a most hasty retreat before the father, with a long red "hide" in his hand, could reach the door. The man grimaced, declaring, could he have his way, every black in the country would be sold away to labor.

Finding the house of his friend, he was safely secluded until evening, when developing his scheme, the old material extinguished and left to mould and rot after the demonstration at Southampton, was immediately rekindled, never again to be suppressed until the slaves stood up the equal of the masters. Southampton—the name of Southampton to them was like an electric shock.

"Ah, Laud!" replied Uncle Medly, an old man of ninety-four years, when asked whether or not he would help his brethren in a critical time of need. "Dat I would. Ef I do noffin' else, I pick up dirt an' tro' in der eye!" meaning in that of their masters.

"Glory to God!" exclaimed his wife, an old woman of ninety years.

"Hallelujah!" responded her daughter, the wife of Norton, the man of the house.

"Blessed be God's eternal name!" concluded the man himself. "I've long been praying and looking, but God has answered me at last."

"None could answer it, but a prayer-hearing God!" replied the wife.

"None would answer it, but a prayer-hearing God!" responded the husband.

"None did answer it, but a prayer-hearing God!" exclaimed the woman. "Glory to God! Glory to God! 'Tis none but He can deliver!"

They fell on their knees to pray, when fervent was their devotion; after which Henry left, but on account of a strict existing patrol regulation, was obliged for three days to be in the wood, so closely watched was he. The fourth evening he effected most adroitly an escape from his hiding place, passing through a strong guard of patrol all around him, entering the District of Columbia at early dawn, soon entering the City of Washington.

The slave prison of Williams and Brien conspicuously stood among the edifices; high in the breeze from the flagstaff floated defiantly the National Colors, stars as the pride of the white man, and stripes as the emblem of power over the blacks. At this the fugitive gave a passing glance, but with hurried steps continued his course, not knowing whither he would tarry. He could only breathe in soliloquy, "How long, O Lord of the oppressed, how long shall this thing continue?"

Passing quietly along, gazing in at every door, he came to a stop on the corner of Pennsylvania avenue and Sixth Street. On entering, looking into the establishment, his eye unexpectedly caught that of a person who proved to be a mulatto gentleman, slowly advancing toward the door.

His first impulse was to make a retreat, but fearing the effort would be fatal, bracing his nerves, he stood looking the person full in the face.

"Do you want anything, young man?" enquired the mulatto gentleman, who proved to be the proprietor.

"I am hungry, sir!" Henry quickly replied.

"You're a stranger, then, in the city?"

"I am, sir."

"Never here before?"

"Never before, sir."

"Have you no acquaintance in the place?"

"None at all, sir."

"Then, sir, if you'll come in, I'll see if I can find as much as you can eat." replied the goodhearted man.

Setting him down to a comfortable breakfast, the wife and niece of the proprietor kindly attended upon him, filling his pouch afterwards with sufficient for the day's travel.

Giving him a parting hand, Henry left with, "God Almighty bless the family!" clearing the city in a short time.

"I understand it all," replied the gentleman in response, "and may the same God guide and protect you by the way!" justly regarding him as a fugitive.

The kindness received at the hands of this family brought tears of gratitude to the eyes of the recipient, especially when remembering his treatment from the same class in Charleston and Richmond. About the same time that Henry left the city, the slave of a distinguished Southern statesman also left Washington and the comforts of home and kindness of his master forever.

From Washington taking a retrograde course purposely to avoid Maryland, where he learned they were already well advised and holding gatherings, the margin of Virginia was cut in this hasty passage, so as to reach more important points for communication. Stealing through the neighborhood and swimming the river, a place was reached called Mud Fort, some four miles distant from Harper's Ferry, situated on the Potomac.

Seeing a white man in a field near by, he passed on as if unconscious of his presence, when the person hailing him in broken English questioned his right to pass.

"I am going to Charleston, sir." replied Henry.

"Vat fahr?" inquired the Dutchman.

"On business," replied he.

"You nagher, you! dat ish not anzer mine question! I does ax you vat fahr you go to Charleston, and you anzer me dat!"

"I told you, sir, that I am going on business."

"You ish von zaucy nagher, andt I bleve you one runaway! Py ching, I vill take you pack!" said the man instantly climbing the fence to get into the road where the runaway stood.

"That will do," exclaimed Henry, "you are near enough—I can bring you down there," at the same time presenting a well-charged six-barrel weapon of death; when the affrighted Dutchman fell on the opposite side of the fence unharmed, and Henry put down his weapon without a fire.

Having lurked till evening in a thicket near by, Charleston was entered near the depot, just at the time when the last train was leaving for Washington. Though small, this place was one of the most difficult in which to promote his object, as the slaves were but comparatively few, difficult to be seen, and those about the depot and house servants, trained to be suspicious and mistrustful of strange blacks, and true and faithful to their masters. Still, he was not remiss in finding a friend and a place for the seclusion.

This place was most admirably adapted for the gathering, being held up a run or little stream, in a bramble thicket on a marshy meadow of the old Brackenridge estate, but a few minutes walk from the town. This evening was that of a strict patrol watch, their headquarters for the night being in Worthington's old mills, from which ran the race, passing near which was the most convenient way to reach the place of gathering for the evening.

While stealthily moving along in the dark, hearing a cracking in the weeds and a soft tramping of feet, Henry secreted himself in a thick high growth of Jamestown weeds along the fence, when he slightly discerned a small body of men as if reconnoitering the neighborhood. Sensible of the precariousness of his condition, the fugitive lie as still as death, lest by dint he might be discovered, as much fear and apprehension then prevaded the community.

Charleston, at best, was a hard place for a Negro, and under the circumstances, had he been discovered, no plea would have saved him. Breathlessly crouched beneath the foliage and thorns of the fetid weed, he was startled by a voice suddenly exclaiming—

"Hallo there! who's that?" which provided to be that of one of the patrol, the posse having just come down the bank of the race from the mill.

"Sahvant, mausta!" was the humble reply.

"Who are you?" further enquired the voice.

"Zack Parker, sir."

"Is that you, old Zack?"

"Yes, mausta—honner bright."

"Come, Zack, you must go with us! Don't you know that Negroes are not allowed to be out at night alone, these times? Come along!" said Davy Hunter.

"Honner bright, maus Davy—honner bright!" continued the old black slave of Colonel Davenport, quietly walking beside them along the mill race, the water of which being both swift and deep. "Maus Davy, I got some mighty good rum here in dis flas'—you gentmen hab some? Mighty good! Mine I tells you, maus Davy—mighty good!"

"Well, Zack, we don't care to take a little," replied Bob Flagg. "Have you had your black mouth to this flask?"

"Honner bright, maus Bobby—honner bright!" replied the old man.

Hunter raised the flask to his mouth, the others gathering around, each to take a draught in turn, when instantly a plunge in the water was heard, and the next moment old Zack Parker was swinging his hat in triumph on the opposite bank of the channel, exclaiming, "Honner bright, gentmen! Honner bright! Happy Jack an' no trouble!"—the last part of the sentence being a cant phrase commonly in use in that part of the country, to indicate a feeling free from all cares.

In a rage the flask was thrown in the dark, and alighted near his feet upright in the tufts of grass, when the old man in turn seizing the vessel, exclaiming aloud, "Yo' heath, gentmen! Yo' good heath!" Then turning it up to his mouth, the sound heard across the stream gave evidence of his enjoyment of the remainder of the contents. "Thank'e, gentmen—

good night!" when away went Zack to the disappointment and even amusement of the party.

Taking advantage of this incident, Henry, under a guide, found a place of seclusion, and a small number of good willing spirits ready for the counsel.

"Mine, my chile!" admonished old Aunt Lucy. "Mine hunny, how yeh go long case da all'as lookin' arter black folks."

Taking the nearest course through Worthington's woods, he reached in good time that night the slave quarters of Captain Jack Briscoe and Major Brack Rutherford. The blacks here were united by the confidential leaders of Moore's people, and altogether they were rather a superior gathering of slaves to any yet met with in Virginia. His mission here soon being accomplished, he moved rapidly on to Slaughter's, Crane's and Washington's old plantations, where he caused a glimmer of light, which until then had never been thought of, much less seen, by them.

The night rounds of the patrol of the immediate neighborhood, caused a hurried retreat from Washington's—the last place at which he stopped—and daybreak the next morning found him in near proximity to Winchester, when he sought and obtained a hiding place in the woods of General Bell.

The people here he found ripe and ready for anything that favored their redemption. Taylor's, Logan's, Whiting's and Tidball's plantations all had crops ready for the harvest.

"An' is dis de young man," asked Uncle Talton, stooped with the age of eighty-nine years, "dat we hearn so much ob, dat's gwine all tru de country 'mong de black folks? Tang God a'mighty for wat I lib to see!" and the old man straightened himself up to his greatest height, resting on his staff, and swinging himself around as if whirling on the heel as children sometimes do, exclaimed in the gladness of his heart and the bouyancy of his spirits at the prospect of freedom before him: "I dont disagard none on 'em," referring to the whites.

"We have only 'regarded' them too long, father," replied Henry with a sigh of sorrow, when he looked upon the poor old time and care-worn slave, whose only hope for freedom rested in his efforts.

"I neber 'spected to see dis! God bless yeh, my son! May God 'long yeh life!" continued the old man, the tears streaming down his cheeks.

"Amen!" sanctioned Uncle Ek.

"God grant it!" replied Uncle Duk.

"May God go wid yeh, my son, wheresomeber yeh go!" exclaimed the old slaves present; when Henry, rising from the block of wood upon which he sat, being moved to tears, reaching out his hand, said, "Well, brethren, mothers, and fathers! My time with you is up, and I must leave you—farewell!" when this faithful messenger of his oppressed brethren, was soon in the woods, making rapid strides towards Western Virginia.

Wheeling, in the extreme Western part of Virginia, was reached by the fugitive, where the slaves, already restless and but few in number in consequence of their close proximity to a free state—Ohio being on the opposite side of the river, on the bank of which the town is situated—could never thereafter become contented.

The "Buckeye State" steamer here passed along on a downward trip, when boarding her as a black passenger, Cincinnati in due season was reached, when the passengers were transferred to the "Telegraph No. 2," destined for Louisville, Kentucky. Here crowding in with the passengers, he went directly to Shippenport, a small place but two miles below—the rapids or falls preventing the large class of steamers from going thence except at the time of high water—the "Crystal Palace," a beautiful packet, was boarded, which swiftly took him to Smithland, at the confluence of the Cumberland and Ohio rivers.

From this point access up the Cumberland was a comparatively easy task, and his advent into Nashville, Tennessee, was as unexpected at this time to the slaves, as it was portentous and ominous to the masters.

There was no difficulty here in finding a seclusion, and the introduction of his subject was like the application of fire to a drought-seasoned stubble field. The harvest was ripe and ready for the scythe, long before the reaper and time for gathering came. In both town and country the disappointment was sad, when told by Henry that the time to strike had not yet come; that they for the present must "Stand still and see the salvation!"

"How long, me son, how long we got wait dis way?" asked Daddy Luu, a good old man and member of a Christian church for upwards of forty years.

"I can't tell exactly, father, but I suppose in this, as in all other good works, the Lord's own annointed time!" replied he.

"An' how long dat gwine be, honey? case I's mighty ti'ed waitin' dis way!" earnestly responded the old man.

"I can't tell you how long, father; God knows best."

"An' how we gwine know w'en 'E is ready?"

"When we are ready, He is ready, and not till then is His time."

"God sen we was ready, now den!" concluded the old man, blinded with tears, and who, from the reverence they had for his age and former good counsel among them, this night was placed at the head of the Gathering.

CARRYING WITH HIM THE PRAYERS and blessings of his people here, Henry made rapid strides throughout this state, sowing in every direction seeds of the crop of a future harvest.

From Tennessee Henry boldly strode into Kentucky, and though there seemed to be a universal desire for freedom, there were few who were willing to strike. To run away, with them, seemed to be the highest conceived idea of their right to liberty. This they were doing, and would continue to do on every favorable opportunity, but their right to freedom by self-resistance, to them was forbidden by the Word of God. Their hopes were based on the long-talked-of promised emancipation in the state.

"What was your dependence," inquired he of an old man verging on the icy surface of ninety winters' slippery pathways, "before you had this promise of emancipation?"

"Wy, dar war Guvneh Metcalf, I sho 'e good to black folks," replied Uncle Winson.

"Well, uncle, tell me, supposing he had not been so, what would you have then done?"

"Wy, chile, I sho 'e raise up dat time 'sides dem maus Henry and maus John."

"But what good have they ever done you? I don't see that you are any better off than had they never lived."

"Ah, chile! Da good to we black folks," continued the old man, with a fixed belief that they were emancipationists and the day of freedom, to the slaves drew near.

Satisfied that self-reliance was the furthest from their thoughts, but impressing them with new ideas concerning their rights, the great-hearted runaway bid them "Good bye, and may God open your eyes to see your own condition!" when in a few minutes Lexington was relieved of an enemy, more potent than the hostile bands of red men who once defied the military powers of Kentucky.

In a few days this astonishing slave was again on the smooth waters of the beautiful Ohio, making speed as fast as the steamer "Queen of the West" could carry him down stream towards Grand Gulf on the great river of the Southwest.

Chapter 26

RETURN TO MISSISSIPPI

The evening, for the season, was very fine; the sky beautiful; the stars shining unusually bright; while Henry, alone on the hurricane deck of the "Queen of the West," stood in silence abaft the wheel-house, gazing intently at the golden orbs of Heaven. Now shoots a meteor, then seemingly shot a comet, again glistened a brilliant planet which almost startled the gazer; and while he yet stood motionless in wonder looking into the heavens, a blazing star whose scintillations dazzled the sight, and for the moment bewildered the mind, was seen apparently to vibrate in a manner never before observed by him.

At these things Henry was filled with amazement, and disposed to attach more than ordinary importance to them, as having an especial bearing in his case; but the mystery finds interpretation in the fact that the emotions were located in his own brain, and not exhibited by the orbs of Heaven.

Through the water plowed the steamer, the passengers lively and mirthful, sometimes amusingly noisy, whilst the adventurous and heart-stricken fugitive, without a companion or friend with whom to share his grief and sorrows, and aid in untangling his then deranged mind, threw himself in tribulation upon the humble pallet assigned him, there to pour out his spirit in communion with the Comforter of souls on high.

The early rising of the passengers aroused him from apparently an abridged night of intermitting sleep, when creeping away into a by-place, he spent the remainder of the day. Thus by sleeping through the day, and watching in the night—induced by the proximity to his old home—did the runaway spend the time during the first two days of his homeward journey.

Falling into a deep sleep early on the evening of the third day, he was suddenly aroused about eleven o'clock by the harsh singing of the black firemen on the steamer:

> *Natchez under the Hill!*
> *Natchez under the Hill!*

sung to an air with which they ever on the approach of a steamer, greet the place, as seemingly a sorrowful reminiscence of their ill-fated brethren continually sold there; when springing to his feet and hurrying upon deck, he found the vessel full upon the wharf boat stationed at the Natchez landing.

Taking advantage of the moment—passing from the wheelhouse down the ladder to the lower deck—thought by many to have gone forever from the place, Henry effected without detection an easy transit to the wharf, and from thence up the Hill, where again he found himself amid the scenes of his saddest experience, and the origination and organization of the measures upon which were based his brightest hopes and expectations for the redemption of his race in the South.

Chapter 27

A Night of Anxiety

On Saturday evening, about half past seven, was it that Henry dared again to approach the residence of Colonel Franks. The family had not yet retired, as the lights still burned brilliantly in the great house, when, secreted in the shrubbery contiguous to the hut of Mammy Judy and Daddy Joe, he lay patiently awaiting the withdrawal in the mansion.

"There's no use in talkin', Andy, he's gittin' suspicious of us all," said Charles, "as he threatens us all with the traders; an' if Henry don't come soon, I'll have to leave anyhow! But the old people, Andy, I can't think of leavin' them!"

"Do you think da would go if da had a chance, Charles?"

"Go? yes 'ndeed, Andy, they'd go this night if they could git off. Since the sellin' of Maggie, and Henry's talkin' to 'em, and his goin' an' takin' little Joe, and Ailcey, an' Cloe, an' Polly an' all clearin' out, they altered their notion about stayin' with ole Franks."

"Wish we could know when Henry's comin' back. Wonder what 'e is," said Andy.

"Here!" was the reply in a voice so cautiously suppressed, and so familiarly distinct that they at once recognized it to be that of their long-absent and most anxiously looked-for friend. Rushing upon him, they mutually embraced, with tears of joy and anxiety.

"How have you been anyhow, Henry?" exclaimed Charles in a suppressed tone. "I's so glad to see yeh, dat I ain't agwine to speak to yeh, so I ain't!" added Andy.

"Come, brethren, to the woods!" said Henry; when the three went directly to the forest, two and half miles from the city.

"Well now, Henry, tell us all about yourself. What you been doin'?" inquired Charles.

"I know of nothing about myself worth telling," replied he.

"Oh, pshaw! wot saut a way is dat, Henry; yeh wont tell a body nothin'. Pshaw, dats no way," grumbled Andy.

"Yes, Andy, I've much to tell you; but not of myself; 'tis about our poor oppressed people everywhere I've been! But we have not now time for that."

"Why, can't you tell us nothin'?"

"Well, Andy, since you must have something, I'll tell you this much: I've been in the Dismal Swamp among the High Conjurors, and saw the heads, old Maudy Ghamus and Gamby Gholar."

"Hoop! now 'e's a talkin'! Ef 'e wasn't I wouldn't tell yeh so! An' wat da sa to yeh, Henry?"

"They welcomed me as the messenger of their deliverance; and as a test of their gratitude, made me a High Conjuror after their own order."

"O pshaw, Henry! Da done what? Wy, ole feller, yeh is high sho 'nough!"

"What good does it do, Henry, to be a conjuror?" inquired Charles.

"It makes the more ignorant slaves have greater confidence in, and more respect for, their headmen and leaders."

"Oh yes, I see now! Because I couldn't see why you would submit to become a conjuror if it done no good."

"That's it, Charles! As you know, I'll do anything not morally wrong, to gain our freedom; and to effect this, we must take the slaves, not as we wish them to be, but as we really find them to be."

"You say it gives power, Henry; is there any reality in the art of conjunction?"

"It only makes the slaves afraid of you if you are called a conjuror, that's all!"

"Oh, I understand it well enough now!" concluded Charles.

"I undehstood well 'nough fuss, but I want to know all I could, dat's all!" added Andy. "Ole Maudy's a high feller, aint 'e, Henry?"

"Oh yes! he's the Head," replied Charles.

"No," explained Henry, "he's not now Head, but Gamby Gholar, who has for several years held that important position among them. Their Council consists of Seven, called the 'Heads,' and their Chief is called 'the Head.' Everything among them, in religion, medicine, laws, or politics, of a public character, is carried before the Head in Council to be settled and disposed of."

"Now we understan'," said Andy, "but tell us, Henry, how yeh get 'long 'mong de folks whar yeh bin all dis time?"

"Very well; everywhere except Kentucky, and there you can't move them toward a strike!"

"Kentucky!" rejoined Andy. "I all'as thought dat de slaves in dat state was de bes' treated uv any, an' dat da bin all 'long spectin' to be free."

"That's the very mischief of it, Andy! 'Tis this confounded 'good treatment' and expectation of getting freed by their oppressors, that has been the curse of the slave. All shrewd masters, to keep their slaves in check, promise them their freedom at their, the master's death, as though they were certain to die first. This contents the slave, and makes him obedient and willing to serve and toil on, looking forward to the promised redemption. This is just the case precisely now in Kentucky. It was my case. While Franks treated me well, and made promises of freedom to my wife"—and he gave a deep sigh—"I would doubtless have been with him yet; but his bad treatment—his inhuman treatment of my wife—my poor, poor wife!—poor Maggie! was that which gave me courage, and made me determined to throw off the yoke, let it cost me what it would. Talk to me of a good master! A 'good master' is the very worst of masters. Were they all cruel and inhuman, or could the slaves be made to see their treatment aright, they would not endure their oppression for a single hour!"

"I sees it, I sees it!" replied Andy.

"An' so do I," added Charles, "who couldn't see that?"

"I tells yeh, Henry, it was mighty haud for me to make up my mine to leave ole Potteh; but even sence you an' Chaules an' me made de vow togedder, I got mo' an' mo' to hate 'im. I could chop 'is head off sometime, I get so mad. I bleve I could chop off Miss Mary' head; an' I likes hur; she mighty good to we black folks."

"Pshaw! yes 'ndeed' ole Frank's head would be nothin' for me to chop off; I could chop off mistess head, an' you know she's a good woman; but I mus' be mighty mad fus'!" said Charles.

"That's it, you see. There is no danger that a 'good' master or mistress will ever be harmed by the slaves. There's neither of you, Andy, could muster up courage enough to injure a 'good master' or mistress. And even I now could not have the heart to injure Mrs. Franks," said Henry.

"Now me," replied Charles.

"Yes, 'ndeed, dats a fac', case I knows I couldn' hurt Miss Mary Potteh. I bleve I'd almos' chop off anybody's head if I see 'em 'tempt to hurt 'e!" added Andy; when they heartily laughed at each other.

"Just so!" said Henry. "A slave has no just conception of his own wrongs. Had I dealt with Franks as he deserved, for doing that for which he would have taken the life of any man had it been his case—tearing my wife from my bosom!—the most I could take courage directly to do, was to leave him, and take as many from him as I could induce to go. But maturer reflection drove me to the expedient of avenging the general wrongs of our people, by inducing the slave, in his might, to scatter red ruin throughout the region of the South. But still, I cannot find it in my heart to injure an individual, except in personal conflict."

"An has yeh done it, Henry?" earnestly inquired Andy.

"Yes, Andy; yes, I have done it! and I thank God for it! I have taught the slave that mighty lesson: to strike for Liberty. 'Rather to die as freemen, than live as slaves!'"

"Thang God!" exclaimed Charles.

"Amen!" responded Andy.

"Now, boys, to the most important event of your lives!" said Henry.

"Wat's dat?" asked Andy.

"Why, get ready immediately to leave your oppressors tonight!" replied he.

"Glory to God!" cried Andy.

"Hallelujah!" responded Charles.

"Quietly! Softly! Easy, boys, easy!" admonished Henry, when the party in breathless silence, on tiptoe moved off from the thicket in which they were then seated, toward the city.

It was now one o'clock in the night, and Natchez shrouded in darkness and quiet, when the daring and fearless runaway with his companions, entered the enclosure of the great house grounds, and approaced the door of the hut of Daddy Joe and Mammy Judy.

"Who dat! Who dat, I say? Ole man, don' yeh hear some un knockin' at de doh?" with fright said Mammy Judy in a smothered tone, hustling and nudging the old man, who was in a deep sleep, when Henry rapped softly at the door.

"Wat a mautta, ole umin?" after a while inquired the old man, rubbing his eyes.

"Some un at de doh!" she replied.

"Who dar?" inquired Daddy Joe.

"A friend!" replied Henry with suppressed voice.

"Ole man, open de doh quick! I bleve in me soul dat Henry! Open de doh!" said mammy.

On the door being opened, the surprise and joy of the old woman was only equalled by the emotion of her utterance.

"Dar! dar now, ole man! I tole 'em so, but da 'uden bleve me! I tole 'em 'e comin', but da 'uden lis'en to me! Did yeh git 'er, me son? Little Joe cum too? O Laud! whar's my po' chile! What's Margot?"

To evade further inquiry, Henry replied that they were all safe, and hoping to see her and the old man.

"How yeh bin, my chile? I'se glad to see yeh, but mighty sorry eh cum back; case de wite folks say, da once git der hands on yeh da neber let yeh go 'g'in! Potteh, Craig, Denny, and all on 'em, da tryin' to fine whar yeh is, hunny!"

"I am well, mammy, and come now to see what is to be done with you old people," said Henry.

"We 'ont to be hear long, chile; de gwine sell us all to de traders!" replied mammy with a deep sigh.

"Yes chile," added Daddy Joe, "we all gwine to de soul-driveh!"

"You'll go to no soul-drivers!" replied Henry, the flash of whose eyes startled Mammy Judy.

"How yeh gwine help it, chile?" kindly asked Daddy Joe.

"I'll show you. Come, come, mammy! You and daddy get ready, as I've come to take you away, and must be at the river before two o'clock," said Henry, who with a single jerk of a board in the floor of the hut, had reached the hidden treasure of the old people.

"Who gwine wid us, chile?" inquired Mammy Judy.

"Charles, Andy, and his female friend, besides some we shall pick up by the way!" replied Henry.

"Now he's a-talkin'!" jocosely said Charles, looking at Andy with a smile, at the mention of his female friend.

"'E ain' doin' nothin' else!" replied Andy.

"Wat become o' po' little Tony! 'E sleep here tonight case he not berry well. Po' chile!" sighed the old woman.

"We'll take him too, of course; and I would that I could take every slave in Natchez!" replied Henry. "It is now half-past one," said he, looking at his watch, "and against two we must be at the river. Go Andy, and get your friend, and meet us at the old burnt sycamore stump above the ferry. Come mammy and daddy, not a word for your lives!" admonished Henry, when taking their package on his back, and little Tony by the hand, they left forever the great house premises of Colonel Stephen Franks in Natchez.

On approaching the river a group was seen, which proved to consist of Andy, Clara (to whom his integrity was plighted), and the faithful old stump, their guidepost for the evening. Greeting each other with tears of joy and fearful hearts, they passed down to the water's edge, but a few hundred feet below.

The ferry boat in this instance was a lightly built yawl, commanded by a white man; the ferry one of many such selected along the shore, expressly for such occasions.

"Have you a pass?" demanded the boatman as a ruse, lest he might be watched by a concealed party. "Let me see it!"

"Here, sir," said Henry, presenting to him by the light of a match which he held in his hand for the purpose, the face of a half eagle.

"Here is seven of you, an' I can't do it for that!" in an humble undertone supplicating manner, said the man. "I axes that for one!"

The weight of seven half eagles dropped into his hand, caused him eagerly to seize the oars, making the quickest possible time to the opposite side of the river.

Chapter 28

STUDYING HEAD WORK

"Now Henry," said Andy, after finding themselves in a safe place some distance from the landing, "you promise' w'en we stauted to show us de Noth Star—which is it?" On looking up the sky was too much obscured with clouds.

"I can't show it to you now, but when we stop to refresh, I'll then explain it to you," replied he.

"It high time now, chil'en, we had a mou'full to eat ef we got travel dis way!" suggested Mammy Judy, breaking silence for the first time since they left the great house.

"Yes," replied Andy, "Clara and little Tony mus' wan' to eat, an' I knows wat dis chile wants!" touching himself on the breast.

The runaways stopped in the midst of an almost impenetrable thicket, kindled a fire to give them light, where to take their fare of cold meat, bread and butter, and cheese, of which the cellar and pantry of Franks, to which Mammy Judy and Charles had access, afforded an ample supply.

Whilst the others were engaged in refreshing, Henry, aside of a stump, was busily engaged with pencil and paper.

"Whar's Henry, dat 'e ain't hear eatin?" inquired Mammy Judy, looking about among the group.

"I sho, ole umin, 'e's oveh dar by de stump," replied Daddy Joe.

"Wat dat boy doin' dar? Henry, wat yeh doin'? Mus' be studyin' headwuck, I reckon! Sho boy! betteh come 'long an' git a mou'full to eat. Yeh ain' hungry I reckon," said the old woman.

"Henry, we dun eatin' now. You mos' ready to tell us 'bout de Noth Star?" said Andy.

"Yes, I will show you," said Henry, walking forward and setting himself in the center of the group. "You see these seven stars which I've drawn on this piece of paper—numbered 1, 2, 3, 4, 5, 6, 7? From the peculiarity of the shape of their relative position to each other, the group is called the 'Dipper,' because to look at them they look like a dipper or a vessel with a long handle.

"I see it; don't you see dat, Chaules?" said Andy.

"Certainly, anybody could see that," replied Charles.

"Ole umin," said Daddy Joe, "don' yeh see it?"

"Sho', ole man! Ain't I lookin!" replied the old woman.

"You all see it then, do you?" inquired Henry.

"Yes, yes!" was the response.

"Now then," continued Henry; "for an explanation by which you can tell the North Star, when or from whatever place you may see it. The two stars of the Dipper, numbered 6 and 7, are called the pointers, because they point directly to the North Star, a very small, bright star, far off from the pointers, generally seeming by itself, especially when the other stars are not very bright.

"The star numbered 8, above the pointer, a little to the left, is a dim, small star, which at first sight would seem to be in a direct line with it; but by drawing a line through 7 to 8, leaves a space as you see between the star 6 and lower part of the line; or forms an angle (as the 'book men' call it, Andy) of ten degrees. The star number 9 in the distance, and a little to the right, would also seem to be directly opposite the pointers; but by drawing a line through 7 to 9, there is still a space left between the lower end of the line and 6. Now trace the dotted line from 6 through the center of 7, and it leads directly to 10. This is the North Star, the slave's great Guide to Freedom! Do you all now understand it?"

"See it!" replied Andy. "Anybody can't see dat, ain' got sense' 'nuff to run away, an' no call to be free, dat's all! I knows all about it. I reckon I a'mos' know it betteh dan you, Henry!"

"Dar, dar, I tole yeh so! I tole yeh dat boy studyin' head wuck, an yeh 'uden bleve me! 'E run about yendeh so much an' kick up 'e heel dat'e talk so much gramma an' wot not, dat body haudly undehstan'! I knows dat 'e bin 'splainin do. Ole man, yeh understan' im?" said Mammy Judy.

"Ah, ole umin, dat I does! An' I' been gone forty years 'ago, I' know'd dis much 'bout it!" replied Daddy Joe.

"Above number 2 the second star of the handle of the Dipper, close to it, you will see by steadily looking, a very small star, which I call the knob or thumb-holt of the handle. You may always tell the Dipper by the knob of the handle; and the North star by the Dipper. The Dipper, during the night you will remember, continues to change its position in relation to the earth, so that it sometimes seems quite upside down."

"See here, Henry, does you know all—"

"Stop, Andy, I've not done yet!" interrupted he.

"Uh, heh!" said Andy.

"When the North star cannot be seen," continued Henry, "you must depend alone upon nature for your guide. Feel, in the dark, around the trunks or bodies of trees, especially oak, and whenever you feel moss on the bark, that side on which the moss grows is always to the north. One more explanation and then we'll go. Do you see this little round metallic box? This is called a—"

"Wat dat you call 'talic, Henry? Sho, boy! yeh head so full ob gramma an' sich like dat yeh don' know how to talk!" interrupted Mammy Judy.

"That only means iron or brass, or some hard thing like that, mammy," explained he. "The little box of which I was speaking has in it what is called a compass. It has a face almost like a clock or watch, with one straight hand which reaches entirely across the face, and turns or shakes whenever you move the box. This hand or finger is a piece of metal called 'loadstone' or 'magnet,' and termed the needle of the compass; and this end with the little cross on it, always points in one direction, and that is to the north. See; it makes no difference which way it is moved, this point of the needle turns back and points that way."

"An mus' ye al'as go de way it pints, Henry?" inquired Andy.

"No; not except you are running away from the South to Canada, or the free States; because both of these places are in the north. But when you know which way the north is, you can easily find any other direction you wish. Notice this, all of you."

"When your face is to the north, your back is to the south; your right hand to the east, and your left to the west. Can you remember this?"

"O yes, easy!" replied Andy.

"Then you will always know which way to go, by the compass showing you which is north," explained Henry.

"What does dese letters roun' hear mean, Henry?" further inquired Andy.

"Only what I have already explained; meaning north, east, west, and south, with their intermediate—"

"Dar!" interrupted Mammy Judy. "'E gone into big talk g'in! Sho!"

"Intermediate means between, mammy," explained Henry.

"Den ef dat's it, I lis'en at yeh; case I want gwine bautheh my head wid you' jography an' big talk like dat!" replied the old woman.

"What does a compass cost?" inquired Charles, who had been listening with intense interest and breathless silence at the information given by their much-loved fellow bondman.

"One-half a dollar, or four bits, as we call it, so that every slave who will, may get one. Now, I've told you all that's necessary to guide you from a land of slavery and long suffering, to a land of liberty and future happiness. Are you now all satisfied with what you have learned?"

"Chauls, aint 'e high! See here, Henry, does yeh know all dat yeh tell us? Wy, ole feller, you is way up in de hoobanahs! Wy, you is conjure sho'nuff. Ef I only know'd dis befo', ole Potteh neven keep me a day. O, pshaw! I bin gone long 'go!"

"He'll do!" replied Charles.

"Well, well, well!" apostrophized Mammy Judy. "Dat beats all! Sence I was baun, I nebber hear de like. All along I been tellen on yeh, dat 'e got 'is head chuck cleanfull ob cumbustable, an' all dat, but yeh 'ud'n bleve me! Now yeh see!"

"Ole umin, I 'fess dat's all head wuck! Dat beats Punton! dat boy's nigh up to Maudy Ghamus! Dat boy's gwine to be mighty!" with a deep sigh replied Daddy Joe.

"Come, now, let's go!" said Henry.

On rising from where they had all been sitting with fixed attention upon their leader and his instruction, the sky was observed through the only break in the thicket above their heads, when suddenly they simultaneously exclaimed:

"There's the Dipper! there's the North Star!" all pointing directly to the Godlike beacon of liberty to the American slave.

Leaving Mammy Judy and Daddy Joe, Clara and little Tony, who had quite recovered from his indisposition the early part of the night, in charge of a friend who designedly met them on the Louisiana side of the river, with heightened spirits and a new impulse, Henry, Charles and Andy, started on their journey in the direction of their newly described guide, the North Star.

> *Star of the North thou art not bigger,*
> *Than the diamond in my ring;*
> *Yet every black star-gazing nigger,*
> *Looks up to thee as some great thing!*

was the apostrophe of an American writer to the sacred orb of Heaven, which in this case was fully verified.

During the remainder of the night and next day, being Sabbath, they continued their travel, only resting when overcome wth fatigue.

Continuing in Louisiana by night, and resting by day, Wednesday morning, before daybreak, brought them to the Arkansas river. At first they intended to ford, but like the rivers generally of the South, its depth and other contingencies made it necessary to seek some other means. After consultation in a canebreak, day beginning to dawn, walking boldly up to a man just loosening a skiff from its fastenings, they demanded a passage across the river. This the skiffman refused peremptorily on any pretext, rejecting the sight of a written pass.

"I want none of yer nigger passes!" angrily said he. "They ain't none uv 'em good 'or nothin', no how! It's no use to show it to me, ye's can't git over!"

First looking meaningly and determinedly at Charles and Andy—biting his lips—then addressing himself to the man, Henry said:

"Then I have one that will pass us!" presenting the unmistaking evidence of a shining gold eagle, at the sight of which emblem of his country's liberty, the skiffman's patriotism was at once awakened, and their right to pass as American freemen indisputable.

A few energetic muscular exertions with the oars, and the sturdy boatman promptly landed his passengers on the other side of the river.

"Now, gentlm'n, I done the clean thing, didn't I, by jingo! Show me but half a chance an' I'll ack the man clean out. I dont go in for this slaveholding o' people in these Newnited States uv the South, nohow, so I don't. Dog gone it, let every feller have a fair shake!"

Dropping into his hand the ten-dollar gold piece, the man bowed earnestly, uttering—

"I hope ye's good luck, gent'men! Ye'll al'as fine me ready when ye's come 'long this way!"

Chapter 29

The Fugitives

With much apprehension, Henry and comrades passed hastily through the State of Arkansas, he having previously traversed it partly, had learned sufficient to put him on his guard.

Traveling in the night, to avoid the day, the progress was not equal to the emergency. Though Henry carried a pocket compass, they kept in sight of the Mississippi river, to take their chance of the first steamer passing by.

The third night out, being Monday, at daybreak in the morning, their rest for the day was made at a convenient point within the verge of a forest. Suddenly Charles gave vent to hearty laughter, at a time when all were supposed to be serious, having the evening past, been beset by a train of three Negro-dogs, which, having first been charmed, they slew at the instant; the dogs probably not having been sent on trail of them, but, after the custom of the state, baying on a general round to intimidate the slaves from clandestinely venturing out, and to attack such runaways as might by chance be found in their track.

"Wat's da mauttah, Chauls?" enquired Andy.

"I was just thinking," replied he, "of the sight of three High Conjurers, who if Ghamus and Gholar be true, can do anything they please, having to escape by night, and travel in the wild woods, to evade the pursuit of white men, who do not pretend to know anything about such things."

"Dat's a fack," added Andy, "an' little, scronny triflin' weak, white men at dat—any one uv us heah, ought to whip two or three uv 'em at once. Dares Hugh's a little bit a feller, I could take 'im in one han' an' throw 'im oveh my head, an' ole Pottah, for his pant, he so ole an' good foh nothin, I could whip wid one hand half a dozen like 'im."

"Now you see, boys," said Henry, "how much conjuration and such foolishness and stupidity is worth to the slaves in the South. All that it does, is to put money into the pockets of the pretended conjurer, give him power over others by making them afraid of him; and even old Gamby Gholar and Maudy Ghamus and the rest of the Seven Heads, with all of the High Conjurors in the Dismal Swamp, are depending more upon me to deliver them from their confinement as prisoners in the Swamp and runaway slaves, than all their combined efforts together. I made it a special part of my mission, wherever I went, to enlighten them on this subject."

"I wandah you didn't fend 'em," replied Andy.

"No danger of that, since having so long, to no purpose, depended upon such persons and nonsense, they are sick at heart of them, and waiting willing and ready, for anything which may present for their aid, even to the destruction of their long cherished, silly nonsense of conjuration."

"Thang God foh dat!" concluded Andy.

Charles having fallen asleep, Andy became the sentinel of the party, as it was the arrangement for each one alternately, every two hours during rest, to watch while the other two slept. Henry having next fallen into a doze, Andy heard a cracking among the bushes, when on looking around, two men approached them. Being fatigued, drowsy, and giddy, he became much alarmed, arousing his comrades, all springing to their feet. The men advanced, who, to their gratification proved to be Eli and Ambrose, two Arkansas slaves, who having promised to meet Henry on his return, had effected their escape immediately after first meeting him, lurking in the forest in the direction which he had laid out to take.

Eli was so fair as to be taken, when first seen, to be a white man. Throwing their arms about Henry, they bestowed upon him their blessing and thanks, for his advent into the state as the means of their escape.

While thus exchanging congratulations, the approach upstream of a steamer was heard, and at once Henry devised the expedient, and determined boldly to hail her and demand a passage. Putting Eli forward as the master, Ambrose carrying the portmanteaus which belonged to the two, and the others with bundles in their hands, all rushed to the bank of the river on the verge of the thicket; Eli held up a handkerchief as a signal. The bell tolled, and the yawl immediately lowered, made for the shore. It was agreed that Eli should be known as Major Ely, of Arkansas.

Seeing that blacks were of the company, when the yawl approached, the mate stood upon her forecastle.

"What's the faction here?" cried out the sturdy mate.

"Where are you bound?" enquired Eli.

"For St. Louis."

"Can I get a passage for myself and four Negroes?"

"What's the name, sir?"

"Major Ely, of Arkansas," was the reply.

"Aye, aye, sir, come aboard," said the mate; when, pulling away, the steamer was soon reached, the slaves going to the deck, and the master to the cabin.

On application for a stateroom, the clerk, on learning the name, desired to know his destination.

"The State of Missouri, sir," said Eli, "between the points of the mouth of the Ohio and St. Genevieve."

"Ely," repeated the clerk, "I've heard that name before—it's a Missouri name—any relation to Dr. Ely, Major?"

"Yes, a brother's son," was the prompt reply.

"Yes, yes, I thought I knew the name," replied the clerk. "But the old fellow wasn't quite of your way of thinking concerning Negroes, I believe?"

"No, he is one man, and I'm another, and he may go his way, and I'll go mine," replied Eli.

"That's the right feeling, Major," replied the clerk, "and we would have a much healthier state of politics in the country, if men generally would only agree to act on that principle."

"It has ever been my course," said Eli.

"Peopling a new farm I reckon, Major?"

"Yes, sir."

The master, keeping a close watch upon the slaves, was frequently upon deck among them, and requested that they might be supplied with more than common fare for slaves, he sparing no expense to make them comfortable. The slaves, on their part, appeared to be particularly attached to him, always smiling when he approached, apparently regretting when he left for the cabin.

Meanwhile, the steamer gracefully plowing up the current, making great headway, reached the point desired, when the master and slaves were safely transferred from the steamer to the shore of Missouri.

Chapter 30

The Pursuit

The absence of Mammy Judy, Daddy Joe, Charles, and little Tony, on the return early Monday morning of Colonel Franks and lady from the country, unmistakably proved the escape of their slaves, and the further proof of the exit of 'squire Potter's Andy and Beckwith's Clara, with the remembrance of the stampede a few months previously, required no further confirmation of the fact, when the neighborhood again was excited to ferment. The advisory committee was called into immediate council, and ways and means devised for the arrest of the recreant slaves recently left, and to prevent among them the recurrence of such things; a pursuit was at once commenced, which for the three succeeding days was carried in the wrong direction—towards Jackson, whither, it was supposed in the neighborhood, Henry had been lurking previous to the last sally upon their premises, as he had certainly been seen on Saturday evening, coming from the landing.

No traces being found in that direction, the course was changed, the swiftest steamer boarded in pursuit for the Ohio river. This point being reached but a few hours subsequent to that of the fugitives, when learning of their course, the pursuers proceeded toward the place of their destination, on the Mississippi river.

This point being the southern part of Missouri but a short distance above the confluence of the Ohio and Mississippi, the last named river had, of necessity, to be passed, being to the fugitives only practicable by means of a ferry. The ferryman in this instance commanded a horse-boat, he residing on the opposite side of the river. Stepping up to him—a tall, raw-boned athletic, rough looking, bearded fellow—Eli saluted:

"We want to cross the river, sir!"

"Am yers free?" enquired the ferryman.

"Am I free! Are you free?" rejoined Eli.

"Yes, I be's a white man!" replied the boatman.

"And so am I!" retorted Eli. "And you dare not tell me I'm not."

"I'll swong, stranger, yer mus' 'scuse me, as I did n' take notice on yez! But I like to know if them air black folks ye got wey yer am free, cause if they arn't, I be 'sponsible for 'em 'cording to the new law, called,

I 'bleve the Nebrasky Complimize Fugitive Slave Act, made down at Californy, last year," apologized and explained the somewhat confused ferryman.

"Yes," replied Henry, "we are free, and if we were not, I do'nt think it any part of your business to know. I thought you were here to carry people across the river."

"But frien'," rejoined the man, "yer don't understan' it. This are a law made by the Newnited States of Ameriky, an' I be 'bliged to fulfill it by ketchin' every fugitive that goes to cross this way, or I mus' pay a thousand dollars, and go to jail till the black folks is got, if that be's never. Yer see yez can't blame me, as I mus' 'bey the laws of Congress I'll swong it be's hardly a fair shake nuther, but I be 'bliged to 'bey the laws, yer know."

"Well sir," replied Henry, "we want to cross the river."

"Let me see yez papers frien'?" asked the ferryman.

"My friend," said Henry, "are you willing to make yourself a watch dog for slaveholders, and do for them that which they would not do for themselves, catch runaway slaves? Don't you know that this is the work which they boast on having the poor white men at the North do for them? Have you not yet learned to attend to your own interests instead of theirs? Here are our free papers," holding out his open hand, in which lay five half eagle pieces.

"Jump aboard!" cried the ferryman. "Quick, quick!" shouted he, as the swift feet of four hourses were heard dashing up the road.

Scarcely had the boat moved from her fastenings, till they had arrived; the riders dismounted, who presenting revolvers, declared upon the boatman's life, instantly, if he did not change the direction of his boat and come back to the Missouri shore. Henry seized a well-charged rifle belonging to the boatman, his comrades each with a well-aimed six-barreled weapon.

"Shoot if you dare!" exclaimed Henry, the slaveholders declining their arms—when, turning to the awestricken ferryman, handing him the twenty-five dollars, said, "your cause is a just one, and your reward is sure; take this money, proceed and you are safe—refuse, and you instantly die!"

"Then I be to do right," declared the boatman, "if I die by it," when applying the whip to the horses, in a few moments landed them on the Illinois shore.

This being the only ferry in the neighborhood, and fearing a bribe or coercion by the people on the Illinois side, or the temptation of a high reward from the slave-catchers, Henry determined on eluding, if possible, every means of pursuit.

"What are your horses worth?" enquired he.

"They can't be no use to your frien' case they is both on 'em bline, an' couldn't travel twenty miles a day, on a stretch!"

"Have you any other horses?"

"They be all the horses I got; I gineraly feed a spell this side. I lives over here—this are my feedin' trip," drawled the boatman.

"What will you take for them?"

"Well, frien', they arn't wuth much to buy, no how, but wuth good lock to me for drawin' the boat over, yer see."

"What did they cost you in buying them?"

"Well, I o'ny giv six-seven dollars apiece, or sich a maiter for 'em' when I got 'em, an' they cos me some two-three dollars, or sich a matter, more to get 'em in pullin' order, yer see."

"Will you sell them to me?"

"I hadn't ort to part wey 'em frien', as I do good lock o' bisness hereabouts wey them air nags, bline as they be."

"Here are thirty dollars for your horses," said Henry, putting into his hand the money in gold pieces, when, unhitching them from their station, leading them out to the side of the boat, he shot them, pushing them over into the river.

"Farewell, my friend," saluted Henry, he and comrades leaving the astonished ferryman gazing after them, whilst the slaveholders on the other shore stood grinding their teeth, grimacing their faces, shaking their fists, with various gesticulations of threat, none of which were either heard, heeded or cared for by the fleeting party, or determined ferryman.

Taking a northeasterly course of Indiana, Andy being an accustomed singer, commenced, in lively glee and cheerful strains, singing to the expressive words:

> *We are like a band of pilgrims,*
> *In a strange and foreign land,*
> *With our knapsacks on our shoulders,*
> *And our cudgels in our hands,*
>
> *We have many miles before us.*
> *But it lessens not our joys,*

> *We will sing a merry chorus,*
> *For we are the tramping boys.*

Then joined in chorus the whole party—

> *We are all jogging,*
> *Jog, jog, jogging,*
> *And we're all jogging,*
> *We are going to the North!*

The Wabash river becoming the next point of obstruction, a ferry, as in the last case, had also to be crossed, the boatman residing on the Indiana side.

"Are you free?" enquired the boatman, as the party of blacks approached.

"We are," was the reply of Henry.

"Where are you from?" continued he.

"We are from home, sir," replied Charles, "and the sooner you take us across the river, just so much sooner will we reach it."

Still doubting their right to pass he asked for their papers, but having by this time become so conversant with the patriotism and fidelity of these men to their country, Charles handing the Indianan a five dollar piece, who on seeing the outstretched wings of the eagle, desired no further evidence of their right to pass, conveying them into the state, contrary to the statutes of the Commonwealth.

On went the happy travelers without hinderance, or molestation, until the middle of the week next ensuing.

Chapter 31

The Attack, Resistance, Arrest

The travel for the last ten days had been pleasant, save the necessity in the more southern part of the state, of lying-by through the day and traveling at night—the fugitives cheerful and full of hope, nothing transpiring to mar their happiness, until approaching a village in the center of northern Indiana.

Supposing their proximity to the British Provinces made them safe, with an imprudence not before committed by the discreet runaways, when nearing a blacksmith's shop a mile and a half from the village, Andy in his usual manner, with stentorian voice, commenced the following song:

> *I'm on my way to Canada,*
> *That cold and dreary land:*
> *The dire effects of slavery,*
> *I can no longer stand.*
> *My soul is vexed within me so,*
> *To think that I'm a slave,*
> *I've now resolved to strike the blow,*
> *For Freedom or the grave.*

All uniting in the chorus,

> *O, righteous Father*
> *Wilt thou not pity me;*
> *And aid me on to Canada,*
> *Where fugitives are free?*
> *I heard old England plainly say,*
> *If we would all forsake,*
> *Our native land of Slavery,*
> *And come across the lake.*

"There, Ad'line! I golly, don't you hear that?" said Dave Starkweather, the blacksmith, to his wife, both of whom on hearing the unusual noise of singing, thrust their heads out of the door of a little log hut, stood patiently listening to the song, every word of which they distinctly caught. "Them's fugertive slaves, an' I'll have 'em tuck up; they might have passed, but for their singin' praise to that darned Queen! I can't stan' that no how!"

"No," replied Adaline, "I'm sure I don't see what they sing to her for; she's no 'Merican. We ain't under her now, as we Dave?"

"No we ain't, Ad'line, not sence the battle o' Waterloo, an' I golly, we wouldn't be if we was. The 'Mericans could whip her a darned sight easier now than what they done when they fit her at Waterloo."

"Lah me, Dave, you could whip 'er yourself, she ai'nt bigger nor tother wimin is she?" said Mrs. Starkweather.

"No she ain't, not a darn' bit!" replied he.

"Dave, ask em in the shop to rest," suggested the wife in a hurried whisper, elbowing her husband as the party advanced, having ceased singing so soon as they saw the faces of white persons.

"Travlin', I reckon?" interrogated the blacksmith. "Little tired, I spose?"

"Yes sir, a little so," replied Henry.

"Didn't come far, I 'spect?" continued he.

"Not very," carelessly replied Henry.

"Take seat there, and rest ye little," pointing to a smoothly-worn log, used by the visitors of the shop.

"Thank you," said Henry, "we will," all seating themselves in a row.

"Take little somethin?" asked he; stepping back to a corner, taking out a caddy in the wall, a rather corpulent green bottle, turning it up to his mouth, drenching himself almost to strangulation.

"We don't drink, sir," replied the fugitives.

"Temperance, I reckon?" enquired the smith.

"Rather so," replied Henry.

"Kind o' think we'll have a spell o' weather?"

"Yes," said Andy, "dat's certain; we'll have a spell a weatheh!"

On entering the shop, the person at the bellows, a tall, able-bodied young man, was observed to pass out at the back door, a number of persons of both sexes to come frequently look in, and depart, succeeded by others; no import being attached to this, supposing themselves to be an attraction, partly from their singing, and mainly from their color being a novelty in the neighborhood.

During conversation with the blacksmith, he after eyeing very

MARTIN R. DELANY

closely the five strangers, was observed to walk behind the door, stand for some minutes looking as if reading, when resuming his place at the anvil, after which he went out the back door. Curiosity now, with some anxiety induced Henry to look for the cause of it, when with no little alarm, he discovered a handbill fully descriptive of himself and comrades, having been issued in the town of St. Genevieve, offering a heavy reward, particularizing the scene at the Mississippi ferry, the killing of the horses as an aggravated offense, because depriving a poor man of his only means of livelihood, being designed to strengthen inducements to apprehend them, the bill being signed "John Harris."

Evening now ensuing, Henry and comrades, the more easily to pass through the village without attraction, had remained until this hour, resting in the blacksmith shop. Enquiring for some black family in the neighborhood, they were cited to one consisting of an old man and woman, Devan by name, residing on the other side, a short distance from the village.

"Ye'll fine ole Bill of the right stripe," said the blacksmith knowingly. "Ye needn' be feard o' him. Ye'll fine him and ole Sally just what they say they is; I'll go bail for that. The first log hut ye come to after ye leave the village is thern; jist knock at the door, an' ye'll fine ole Bill an' Sally all right blame if ye don't. Jis name me; tell 'em Dave Starkweather sent ye there, an' blamed if ye don't fine things at high water mark; I'm tellin' ye so, blamed if I ain't!" was the recommendation of the blacksmith.

"Thank you for your kindness," replied Henry, politely bowing as they rose from the log. "Goodbye, sir!"

"Devilish decent lookin' black fellers," said the man of the anvil, complimenting designedly for them to hear. "Blamed if they ain't as free as we is—I golly they is!"

Without, as they thought, attracting attention, passing through the village a half mile or more, they came to a log hut on the right side of the way.

"How yeh do fren? How yeh come on?" saluted a short, rather corpulent, wheezing old black man. "Come in. Hi! Dahs good many on yeh; ole 'omin come, heah's some frens!" calling his wife Sally, an old woman, shorter in stature, but not less corpulent than he, sitting by a comfortable dry-stump fire.

"How is yeh, frens? How yeh do? come to da fiah, mighty cole!" said the old woman.

"Quite cool," replied Andy, rubbing his hands, spreading them out, protecting his face from the heat.

"Yeh is travelin, I reckon, there is good many go' long heah; we no call t'ask 'em whah da gwine, we knows who da is, case we come from dah. I an, ole man once slave in Faginny; mighty good country fah black folks."

Sally set immediately about preparing something to give her guests a good meal. Henry admonished them against extra trouble, but they insisted on giving them a good supper.

Deeming it more prudent, the hut being on the highway, Henry requested to retire until summoned to supper, being shown to the loft attained by a ladder and simple hatchway, the door of which was shut down, and fastened on the lower side.

The floor consisting of rough, unjointed board, containing great cracks through which the light and heat from below passed up, all could be both seen and heard, which transpired below.

Seeing the old man so frequently open and look out at the door, and being suspicious from the movements of the blacksmith and others, Henry affecting to be sleepy, requested Billy and his wife when ready, to awaken them, when after a few minutes, all were snoring as if fast asleep, Henry lying in such a position as through a knothole in the floor, to see every movement in all parts of the room. Directly above him in the rafter within his reach, hung a mowing scythe.

"Now's yeh time, ole man; da all fas' asleep, da snorin' good!" said old Sally, urging Billy to hasten, who immediately left the hut.

The hearts of the fugitives were at once "in their mouths," and with difficulty it was by silently reaching over and heavily pressing upon each of them, Henry succeeded in admonishing each to entire quietness and submission.

Presently entered a white man, who whispering with Sally left the room. Immediately in came old Bill, at the instant of which, Henry found his right hand above him, involuntarily grasped firmly on the snath of the scythe.

"Whah's da?" enquired old Bill, on entering the hut.

"Sho da whah yeh lef' em!" replied the old woman.

"'Spose I kin bring 'em in now?" continued old Bill.

"Bring in who?"

"Da white folks: who else I gwine fetch in yeh 'spose?"

"Bettah let em 'tay whah da is, an' let de po' men lone, git sumpen t' eat, an' go 'long whah da gwine!" replied Sally, deceptively.

"Huccum yeh talk dat way? Sho yeh tole me go!" replied Billy.

"Didn' reckon yeh gwine bring 'em on da po' cretahs dis way, fo' da git moufful t' eat an' git way so."

"How I gwine let 'em go now de white folks all out dah? Say Sally? Dat jis what make I tell yeh so!"

"Bettah let white folks 'lone, Willum! dat jis what I been tellin' on yeh. Keep foolin' 'long wid white folks, bym'by da show yeh! I notrus' white man, no how. Sho! da no fren' o' black folks. Bus spose body 'blige keep da right side on 'em long so."

"Ole 'omin," said Bill, "yeh knows we make our livin' by da white folks, an' mus' do what da tell us, so whah's da use talkin' long so. 'Spose da come in now?"

"Sho, I tole yeh de man sleep? gwine bring white folks on 'em so? give po' cretahs no chance? Go long, do what yeh gwine do; yeh fine out one dese days!" concluded Sally.

Having stealthily risen to their feet standing in a favorable position, Henry in whispers declared to his comrades that with that scythe he intended mowing his way into Canada.

Impatient for their entrance, throwing wide open the door of the hut, which being the signal, in rushed eleven white men, headed by Jud Shirly, constable, Dave Starkweather the blacksmith, and Tom Overton as deputies; George Grove, a respectable well-dressed villager, stood giving general orders.

With light and pistol in hand, Franey, mounting the stairway commanded a surrender. Eli, standing behind the hatchway, struck the candle from his hand, when with a swing of the scythe there was a screech, fall, and groan heard, then with a shout and leap, Henry in the lead, they cleared the stairs to the lower floor, the white men flying in consternation before them, making their way to the village, alarming the inhabitants.

The fugitives fled in great haste continuing their flight for several miles, when becoming worn down and fatigued, retired under cover of a thicket a mile from a stage tavern kept by old Isaac Slusher of German descent.

The villagers following in quick pursuit, every horse which could be readily obtained being put on the chase, the slaves were overtaken, fired upon—a ball lodging in Charles' thigh—overpowered, and arrested. Deeming it, from the number of idlers about the place, and the condition of the stables, much the safest imprisonment, the captives were taken to the tavern of Slusher, to quarter for the night.

On arriving at this place, a shout of triumph rent the air, and a general cry "take them into the barroom for inspection! Hang them! Burn them!" and much more.

Here the captives were derided, scoffed at and ridiculed, turned around, limbs examined, shoved about from side to side, then ordered to sit down on the floor, a noncompliance with which, having arranged themselves for the purpose, at a given signal, a single trip by an equal number of whites, brought the four poor prisoners suddenly to the floor on the broad of their back, their heads striking with great force. At this abuse of helpless men, the shouts of laughter became deafening. It caused them to shun the risk of standing, and keep seated on the floor.

Charles having been wounded, affected inability to stand, but the injury being a flesh wound, was not serious.

"We'll show ye yer places, ye black devils!" said Ned Bradly, a rowdy, drawing back his foot to kick Henry in the face, as he sat upon the floor against the wall, giving him a slight kick in the side as he passed by him.

"Don't do that again, sir!" sternly said Henry, with an expression full of meaning, looking him in the face.

Several feet in an instant were drawn back to kick, when Slusher interfering, said, "Shendlemans! tem black mans ish prishners! You tuz pring tem into mine housh, ant you shandt puse tem dare!" when the rowdies ceased abusing them.

"Well, gentlemen," said Tom Overton, a burly, bullying barroom person, "we'd best git these blacks out of the way, if they's any fun up tonight."

"I cot plendy peds, shendlemans, I ondly vants to know who ish to bay me," replied Slusher.

"I golly," retorted Starkweather, "you needn't give yourself no uneasiness about that Slusher. I think me, and Shirly, and Grove is good for a night's lodging for five niggers, anyhow!"

"I'm in that snap, too!" hallooed out Overton.

"Golly! Yes, Tom, there's you we like to forgot, blamed if we didn't!" responded Starkweather.

"Dat ish all right nough zo far as te plack man's ish gonzern, put ten dare ish to housh vull o' peoples, vot vare must I gheep tem?"

"We four," replied Grove, "will see you paid, who else? Slusher, we want it understood, that we four stand responsible for all expenses incurred this night, in the taking of these Negroes," evidently expecting to receive as they claimed, the reward offered in the advertisement.

"Dat vill too, ten," replied Slusher. "Vell, I ish ready to lite tese black mans to ped."

"No Slusher," interrupted Grove, "that's not the understanding, we don't pay for beds for niggers to sleep in!"

"No, by Molly!" replied Overton. "Dogged if that ain't going a leetle too far! Slusher, you can't choke that down, no how you can fix in. If you do as you please with your own house, these niggers is in our custody, and we'll do as we please with them. We want you to know that we are white men, as well as you are, and can't pay for niggers to sleep in the same house with ourselves."

"Gents," said Ned Bradly, "do you hear that?"

"What?" enquired several voices.

"Why, old Slusher wants to give the niggers a room upstairs with us!"

"With who?" shouted they.

"With us white men."

"No, blamed if he does!" replied Starkweather.

"We won't stand that!" exclaimed several voices.

"Where's Slusher?" enquired Ben West, a discharged stage driver, who hung about the premises, and now figured prominently.

"Here ish me, shendlemans!" answered Slusher, coming from the back part of the house. "Andt you may do as you please midt tem black mans, pud iv you dempt puse me, I vill pudt you all out mine housh!"

"The stable, the stable!" they all cried out. "Put the niggers in the stable, and we'll be satisfied!"

"Tare ish mine staple—you may pud tem vare you blease," replied the old man, "budt you shandt puse me!"

Securely binding them with cords, they were placed in a strongly built log stable closely weather-boarded, having but a door and window below, the latter being closely secured, and the door locked on the outside with a staple and padlock. The upper windows being well secured, the blacks thus locked in, were left to their fate, whilst their captors comfortably housed, were rioting in triumph through the night over the misfortune, and blasted prospects for liberty.

Chapter 32

THE ESCAPE

This night the inmates of the tavern revelled with intoxication; all within the building, save the exemplary family of the stern old German, Slusher, who peremptorily refused from first to last, to take any part whatever with them, doubtless, being for the evening the victims of excessive indulgence in the beverage of ardent spirits. Now and again one and another of the numerous crowd gathered from the surrounding neighborhood, increasing as the intelligence spread, went alone to the stable to examine the door, reconnoiter the premises, and ascertain that the prisoners were secure. The company getting in such high glee that, fearing a neglect of duty, it became advisable to appoint for the evening a corps of sentinels whose special duty, according to their own arrangements, should be to watch and guard the captives. This special commission being one of pecuniary consideration, Jim Franey, the township constable, the rowdy Ned Bradly, and Ben West the discharged stage driver, who being about the premises, readily accepted the office, entering immediately on the line of duty.

The guard each alternately every fifteen minutes went out to examine the premises, when one and a half of the clock again brought around the period of Ben West's duty. Familiar with the premises and the arrangement of the stables, taking a lantern, West designed closely to inspect their pinions, that no lack of duty on his part might forfeit his claim to the promised compensation.

When placing them in the stable, lights then being in requisition, Henry discovered in a crevice between the wall an the end of the feed-trough a common butcher knife used for the purpose of repairing harness. So soon as the parties left the stable, the captives lying with their heads resting on their bundles, Henry arising, took the knife, cutting loose himself and companions, but leaving the pinions still about their limbs as though fastened, resumed his position upon the bundle of straw. The scythe had been carelessly hung on a section of the worm fence adjoining the barn, near the door of the prison department, their weapons having been taken from them.

"Well, boys," enquired West, holding up the lantern, "you're all here,

I see: do you want anything? Take some whiskey!" holding in his hand a quart bottle.

"The rope's too tight around my ankle!" complained Charles. "Its took all the feeling out of my leg."

Dropping upon his knees to loosen the cord, at this moment, Henry standing erect brandishing the keen glistening blade of the knife before him—his companions having sprung to their feet—"Don't you breathe," exclaimed the intrepid unfettered slave, "or I'll bury the blade deep in your bosom! One hour I'll give you for silence, a breach of which will cost your life." Taking a tin cup which West brought into the stable, pouring it full to the brim, "Drink this!" said Henry, compelling the man who was already partially intoxicated, to drink as much as possible, which soon rendered him entirely insensible.

"Come, boys!" exclaimed he, locking the stable, putting the key into his pocket, leaving the intoxicated sentinel prostrated upon the bed of straw intended for them, and leaving the tavern house of the old German Slusher forever behind them.

The next period of watch, West being missed, Ned Bradly, on going to the stable, finding the door locked, reported favorably, supposing it to be still secure. Overton in turn did the same. When drawing near daylight—West still being missed—Franey advised that a search be made for him. The bedrooms, and such places into which he might most probably have retired, were repeatedly searched in vain, as calling at the stable elicited no answer, either from him nor the captives.

The sun was now more than two hours high, and word was received from the village to hasten the criminals in for examination before the magistrate. Determining to break open the door, which being done, Ben West was found outstretched upon the bed of straw, who, with difficulty, was aroused from his stupor. The surprise of the searchers on discovering his condition, was heightened on finding the escape of the fugitives. Disappointment and chagrin now succeeded high hopes and merriment, when a general reaction ran throughout the neighborhood; for the sensation at the escape even became greater than on the instance of the deed of resistance and success of the capture.

Of all the disappointments connected with this affair, there was none to be regretted save that of the old German tavern keeper, Isaac Slusher, who, being the only pecuniary sufferer, the entire crowd revelling at his expense.

"GONVOUND DISH BISHNESH!" EXCLAIMED SLUSHER with vexation. "Id alwaysh cosht more dan de ding ish wordt. Mine Got! afder dish I'll mindt mine own bishnesh. Iv tem Soudt Amerigans vill gheep niggersh de musht gedch dem demzelve. Mine ligger ish ghon, I losht mine resht, te niggersh rhun avay, an' I nod magk von zent!"

Immediate pursuit was sent out in search of the runaways but without success; for, dashing on, scythe in hand, with daring though peaceable strides through the remainder of the state and that of Michigan, the fugitives reached Detroit without further molestation or question from any source on the right of transit, the inhabitants mistaking them for resident blacks out from their homes in search of employment.

Chapter 33

Happy Greeting

After their fortunate escape from the stables of Isaac Slusher in Indiana, Henry and comrades safely landed across the river in Windsor, Essex County, Canada West, being accompanied by a mulatto gentleman resident of Detroit, who from the abundance of his generous heart, with others there, ever stands ready and has proven himself an uncompromising, true and tried friend of his race, and every weary traveler-on a fugitive slave pilgrimage, passing that way.

"Is dis Canada? Is dis de good ole British soil we hear so much 'bout way down in Missierppi?" exclaimed Andy. "Is dis free groun'? De lan' whar black folks is free! Thang God a'mighty for dis privilege!" When he fell upon his hands and knees and kissed the earth.

Poor fellow! he little knew the unnatural feelings and course pursued toward his race by many Canadians, those too pretending to be Englishmen by birth, with some of whom the blacks had fought side by side in the memorable crusade made upon that fairest portion of Her Majesty's Colonial Possessions, by Americans in disguise, calling themselves "Patriots." He little knew that while according to fundamental British Law and constitutional rights, all persons are equal in the realm, yet by a systematic course of policy and artifice, his race with few exceptions in some parts, excepting the Eastern Province, is excluded from the enjoyment and practical exercise of every right, except mere suffrage-voting—even to those of sitting on a jury as its own peer, and the exercise of military duty. He little knew the facts, and as little expected to find such a state of things in the long-talked of and much-loved Canada by the slaves. He knew not that some of high intelligence and educational attainments of his race residing in many parts of the Provinces, were really excluded from and practically denied their rights, and that there was no authority known to the colony to give redress and make restitution on the petition or application of these representative men of his race, which had frequently been done with the reply from the Canadian functionaries that they had no power to reach their case. It had never entered the mind of poor Andy, that in going to Canada in search of freedom, he was then in a country where privileges were denied him which are common to the slave in every Southern state—the right of going into the gallery of a public building—that a few of the most respectable colored ladies of a town in Kent County, desirous through reverence and respect, to see a British Lord Chief Justice on the Bench of Queen's Court, taking seats in the gallery of the court house assigned to females and other visitors, were ruthlessly taken hold of and shown down the stairway by a man and "officer" of the Court of Queen's Bench for that place. Sad would be to him the fact when he heard that the construction given by authority to these grievances, when requested to remedy or remove them, was, that they were "local contingencies to be reached alone by those who inflicted the injuries." An emotion of unutterable indignation would swell the heart of the determined slave, and almost compel him to curse the country of his adoption. But Andy was free—being on British soil—from the bribes of slaveholding influences; where the unhallowed foot of the slavecatcher dare not tread; where no decrees of an American Congress sanctioned by a president born and bred in a free state and himself once a poor apprentice boy in a village, could reach.

Thus far, Andy was happy; happy in the success of their escape, the enlarged hopes of future prospects in the industrial pursuits of life; and happy in the contemplation of meeting and seeing Clara.

There were other joys than those of Andy, and other hopes and anticipations to be realised. Charles, Ambrose, and Eli, who, though with hearts overflowing with gratitude, were silent in holy praise to heaven, claiming to have emotions equal to his, and conjugal expectations quite as sacred if not yet as binding.

"The first thing now to be done is to find our people!" said Henry with emotion, after the excess of Andy had ceased.

"Where are they?" inquired the mulatto gentleman. "And what are their names?"

"Their names at home were Frank's Ailcey, Craig's Polly, and Little Joe, who left several months ago; and an old man and woman called Daddy Joe and Mammy Judy; a young woman called Clara Beckwith, and a little boy named Tony, who came on but a few days before us."

"Come with me, and I'll lead you directly to him!" replied the mulatto gentlemen; when taking a vehicle, he drove them to the country a few miles from Windsor, where the parties under feelings such as never had been experienced by them before, fell into the embrace of each other.

"Dar now, dar! wat I tell you? Bless de laud, ef dar ain' Chaules an'

Henry!" exclaimed Mammy Judy, clapping her hands, giving vent to tears which stole in drops from the eyes of all. "My po' chile! My po' Margot!" continued she in piteous tones as the bold and manly leader pressed closely to his bosom his boy, who now was the image of his mother. "My son, did'n yeh hear nothing bout er? did'n yeh not bring my po' Margot?"

"No, mammy, no! I have not seen and did not bring her! No, mammy, no! But—!" When Henry became choked with grief which found an audible response from the heart of every child of sorrow present.

Clara commenced, seconded by Andy and followed by all except him the pierce to whose manly heart had caused it, in tones the most affecting:

> *O, when shall my sorrow subside!*
> *And when shall my troubles be ended;*
> *And when to the bosom of Christ be conveyed,*
> *To the mansions of joy and bliss!*
> *To the mansions of joy and bliss!*

Falling upon their knees, Andy uttered a most fervent prayer, invoking Heaven's blessing and aid.

"Amen!" responded Charles.

"Hallelujah!" cried Clara, clapping her hands.

"Glory, glory, glory!" shouted Ailcey.

"O laud! W'en shall I get home!" mourned Mammy Judy.

"'Tis good to be here, chilen! 'Tis good to be here!" said Daddy Joe, rubbing his hands quite wet with tears—when all rising to their feet met each other in the mutual embraces of Christian affection, with heaving hearts of sadness.

"We have reason, sir," said Henry addressing himself to the mulatto gentleman who stood a tearful eye witness to the scenes, "we have reason to thank God from the recesses of our hearts for the providential escape we've made from slavery!" which expression was answered only by trickles down the gentleman's cheeks.

The first care of Henry was to invest a portion of the old people's money by the purchase of fifty acres of land with improvements suitable, and provide for the schooling of the children until he should otherwise order. Charles by appointment in which Henry took part, was chosen leader of the runaway party, Andy being the second, Ambrose and Eli respectively the keepers of their money and accounts, Eli being a good penman.

"Now," said Henry, after two days rest, "the time has come and I must leave you! Polly, as you came as the mistress, you must now become the mother and nurse of my poor boy! Take good care of him—mammy will attend to you. Charles, as you have all secured land close to, I want you to stand by the old people; Andy, you, Ambrose, and Eli, stand by Charles and the girls, and you must succeed, as nothing can separate you; your strength depending upon your remaining together."

"Henry, is yeh guine sho' nuff?" earnestly enquired Andy.

"Yes, I must go!"

"Wait little!" replied Andy, when after speaking aside with Eli and Ambrose, calling the girls they all whispered for sometime together; occasional evidence of seriousness, anxiety, and joy marking their expressions of countenance.

The Provincial regulations requiring a license, or three weeks report to a public congregation, and that many sabbaths from the altar of a place of worship to legalise a marriage, and there being now no time for either of these, the mulatto gentleman who was still with them being a clergyman, declared, that in this case no such restrictions were binding; being originally intended for the whites and the free, and not for the panting runaway slave.

"Thank God for that! That's good talk!" said Charles.

"Ef it aint dat, 'taint nothin! Dat's wat I calls good black talk!" replied Andy, causing the clergyman and all to look at each other with a smile.

The party gathered standing in a semicircle, the clergyman in the center, a hymn being sung and prayer offered—rising to their feet, and an exhortation of comfort and encouragement being given, with the fatherly advice and instructions of their domestic guidance in after life by the aged man of God; the sacred and impressively novel words: "I join you together in the bonds of matrimony!" gave Henry the pleasure before leaving of seeing upon the floor together, Charles and Polly, Andy and Clara, Eli and Ailcey, "as man and wife forever."

"Praise God!" exclaimed poor old mammy, whose heart was most tenderly touched by the scene before her, contrasting it by reflection with the sad reminiscence of her own sorrowful and hopeless union with Daddy Joe, with whom she had lived fifty years as happily as was possible for slaves to do.

"Bless de laud!" responded the old man.

MARTIN R. DELANY

The young wives all gave vent to sobs of sympathy and joy, when the parson as a solace sung in touching sentiments:

> *Daughters of Zion! awake from thy sadness!*
> *Awake for they foes shall oppress thee no more.*
> *Bright o'er the hills shines the day star of gladness*
> *Arise! for the night of they sorrow is o'er;*
> *Daughters of Zion, awake from thy sadness!*
> *Awake for they foes shall oppress thee no more!*

"O glory!" exclaimed Mammy Judy, when the scene becoming most affecting; hugging his boy closely to his bosom, upon whose little cheek and lips he impressed kisses long and affectionate, when laying him in the old woman's lap and kissing little Tony, turning to his friends with a voice the tone of which sent through them a thrill, he said:

"By the instincts of a husband, I'll have her if living! If dead, by impulses of a Heaven-inspired soul, I'll avenge her loss unto death! Farewell, farewell!" the tears streaming as he turned from his child and its grandparents; when but a few minutes found the runaway leader seated in a car at the Windsor depot, from whence he reached the Suspension Bridge at Niagara en route for the Atlantic.

Chapter 34

A Novel Adventure

From the Suspension Bridge through the great New York Central Railway to Albany, and thence by the Hudson River, Henry reached the city on the steamer "Hendrick Hudson," in the middle of an afternoon. First securing a boarding house—a new thing to him—he proceeded by direction to an intelligence office, which he found kept by a mulatto gentleman. Here inquiring for a situation as page or valet on a voyage to Cuba, he deposited the required sum, leaving his address as "Gilbert Hopewell, 168 Church St."—changing the name to prevent all traces of himself out of Canada, whither he was known to have gone, to the free states of America, and especially to Cuba whence he was going, the theater of his future actions.

In the evening Henry took a stroll through the great thoroughfare, everything being to him so very novel, that eleven o'clock brought him directly in front of doubtless the handsomest saloon of the kind in the world, situated on the corner of Broadway and Franklin street. Gazing in at the luxurious and fashionable throng and gaieties displayed among the many in groups at the tables, there was one which more than all others attracted his attention, though unconscious at the time of its doing so.

The party consisted of four; a handsome and attractive young lady, accompanied by three gentlemen, all fine looking, attractive persons, wearing the undress uniforms of United States naval officers. The elder of these was a robust, commanding person in appearance, black hair, well mixed with white, seemingly some sixty years of age. One of the young gentlemen was tall, handsome, with raven-black hair, moustache, and eyes; the other, medium height, fair complexion, hair, moustache and whiskers, with blue eyes; while the young lady ranked of medium proportions in height and size, drab hair, fair complexion, plump cheeks and hazel eyes, and neatly dressed in a maroon silk habit, broadly faced in front and cuffed with orange satin, the collar being the same, neatly bound with crimson.

While thus musing over the throng continually passing in and out, unconsciously Henry had his attention so fixed on this group, who were passing out and up Broadway, involuntarily leaving the window through which he had been gazing, he found himself following them in the crowd which throng the street closely, foot to foot.

Detecting himself and about to turn aside, he overheard the elderly gentleman in reply to a question by the lady concerning the great metropolis, say, that in Cuba where in a few days they would be, recreation and pleasure were quite equal to that of New York. Now drawing more closely he learned that the company were destined for Havana, to sail in a few days. His heart beat with joy, when turning and making his way back, he found his boarding house without difficulty.

Henry once more spent a sleepless night, noted by restless anxiety; and the approach of morning seemed to be regulated by the extent of the city. If thoughts could have done it, the great Metropolis would have been reduced to a single block of houses, reducing in like manner the night to a few fleeting moments.

Early in the morning he had risen, and impatiently pacing the floor, imagined that the people of that city were behind the age in rising. Presently the summons came for breakfast, and ere he was seated a note was handed him reading thus:

> Intelligence Office—Leonard St.,
> New York, March 5th, 1853
>
> Gilbert Hopewell
>   There is now an opportunity offered to go to Cuba, to attend on a party of four—a lady and three gentlemen—who sail for Havana direct (see Tribune of this morning). Be at my office at half past ten o'clock, and you will learn particulars, which, by that time I will have obtained.
>   Respectfully, B.A.P.

Though the delay was but an hour, Henry was restless, and when the time came was punctually in his place. The gentleman who called to meet him at the Intelligence office Henry recognized as one of the party seen the previous evening at the great saloon in Broadway. Arrangements having been completed concerning his attendance and going with them, "Meet me in an hour at the St. Nicholas, and commence your duties immediately," said the gentleman, when politely bowing, Henry turned away with a heart of joy, and full of hope.

Promptly to the time he was at the hotel, arranging for a start; when he found that his duties consisted in attendance particularly on the young lady and one of the young gentlemen, and the other two as occasion might require. The company was composed of Captain Richard Paul, the elderly gentleman; Lieutenant Augustus Seeley, the black-haired; passed Midshipman Lawrence Spencer, the light-haired gentleman, and Miss Cornelia Woodward.

Miss Woodward was modest and retiring, though affable, conversant and easy in manner. In her countenance were pictured an expression of definite anxiety and decisive purpose, which commanded for her the regard and esteem of all whom she approached. Proud without vanity, and graceful without affectation, she gained the esteem of everyone; a lady making the remark that she was one of the most perfect of American young ladies.

After breakfast the next morning they embarked on the steam packet "Isabella," to sail that day at eleven o'clock.

Of the gentlemen, Augustus Seeley gave to Miss Woodward the most attention, though nothing in her manner betrayed attachment except an occasional sigh.

Henry, for the time, appeared to be her main dependence; as shortly after sailing she manifested a disposition to keep in retirement as much as possible. Though a girl of tender affections, delicate sentiments, and elevated Christian graces, Cornelia was evidently inexperienced and unprepared for the deceptious impositions practiced in society. Hence, with the highest hopes and expectations, innocently unaware of the contingencies in life's dangerous pathway, hazarding her destiny on the simple promise of an irresponsible young man, but little more than passed midshipman, she reached the quay at Moro Castle in less than six days from the Port of New York.

A Note About the Author

Martin R. Delany (1812–1885) was an abolitionist, writer, soldier, physician, and Black nationalist. Born free in Virginia, Delany was raised in Pittsburgh, Pennsylvania, where he became a physician's assistant and worked tirelessly during the cholera epidemic of 1833. Admitted to Harvard Medical School in 1850, Delany was dismissed after protests by white students threatened his life. After traveling to the South in 1839 to witness the conditions experienced by slaves for the first time, Delany moved to Rochester, New York to work with Frederick Douglass on his abolitionist newspaper *The North Star*. After a brief visit to Liberia and several years in Canada, Delany returned to the United States at the onset of the Civil War, eventually working as a recruiter for the United States Colored Troops and serving as the first African American field grade officer in the Army. During Reconstruction, he moved to South Carolina, where he worked for the Freedmen's Bureau and dedicated himself to activism and politics. Delany was also a prolific pamphleteer, journalist, and novelist whose book *Blake: Or, The Huts of America* (1859–1862) is considered a pioneering work of Black nationalist fiction. Towards the end of his life, Delany devoted himself to the Liberia Exodus Joint Stock Steamship Company, an expedition he envisioned as a response to the growing violence and voter suppression faced by African Americans following the withdrawal of federal troops from the South in 1877. In his final years, Delany returned to his work as a physician, supplementing his wife's income as a seamstress in order to pay for their children to attend Wilberforce College in Ohio.

A Note from the Publisher

bookfinity & ▉ MINT EDITIONS

Enjoy more of your favorite classics with Bookfinity,
a new search and discovery experience for readers.
With Bookfinity, you can discover more vintage
literature for your collection, find your Reader Type,
track books you've read or want to read,
and add reviews to your favorite books.
Visit www.bookfinity.com, and click on
Take the Quiz to get started.

Don't forget to follow us
@bookfinityofficial and @mint_editions

CPSIA information can be obtained
at www.ICGtesting.com
Printed in the USA
JSHW032301150822
29281JS00002B/7

9 781513 296852